FROM THE BOTTOM UP

FROM THE BOTTOM UP

SEAN FLYNN

From The Bottom Up

This is a work of fiction. Names, characters, organizations,
locations, events, and incidents are either products of the
author's imagination or are used fictitiously.

CONTENTS

"You can't get rich in politics unless you're a crook."
- *Harry S. Truman*

"Some rise by sin, and some by virtue fall."
- *William Shakespeare*

"Where there is power, greed, and money, there is corruption."
- *Ken Poirot*

"One politician cannot make a government. He needs accomplices."
- *Ljupka Cvetanova*

"Oftentimes we don't realize we've crossed the line, until we're on the other side of it."
- *Sean Flynn*

PROLOGUE

The blades chopped through the sky and the rotor whirred overhead as a helicopter swooped in a low arc above them on its way inland from the coast. A soft and delicate amber hue held the distant horizon. As the sun dipped into the ocean, the winds stilled. It was an electric night.

Bradford Barnes was a career detective with the LAPD. He'd seen a lot in his time on the force and learned even more. He was an intelligent, committed, and humble man, and tonight, all of those traits came into play as he supported his wife. She was brilliant, he knew this, and this was her time.

Patricia savored the moment and her breath danced in the chill of the tranquil evening air. She was buzzing with life—more alive than she had been in some time. City lights sparkled in the distance as they got into the Range Rover and headed toward downtown. It was a Wednesday evening, so things were more quiet than usual. This was something Patricia had looked forward to for years. The move from special agent to intelligence analyst would take her off the streets and give her what she hoped was the opportunity to stop crimes before they occurred.

Everybody from the local agency would be there. Even folks from the executive level in DC made the trip to celebrate the occasion—her 25 years in service to the bureau. The FBI was a tight-knit family that took care of their own. They reveled in victory and shared their failures. But there was always more work to be done; one thing that made this night of recognition so special.

Having the support of her husband was vital, and she reinforced him in his position as lead detective for the LAPD. They had assisted each other in many cases over the years, and their information exchange helped the department and the bureau to work together effectively.

The drive to the Bonaventure was painstakingly slow despite the mid-week after-hours traffic, and it seemed they hit every light on the way. Although she anticipated the ceremony, the long trek gave her pause to think of the cases she would have to leave behind. Principally the missing persons case that had caused such a commotion over the past few months.

"I'm in a good place, Brad." She adjusted the seat a smidge. "This new promotion should give us some more time together, and with you as the senior detective, things might slow a bit."

"Let's not get our hopes up too high." He smiled, enjoying the idea of a little more time with his wife.

"I must admit, though, I have some reservations over that case you handed me. I hate leaving it behind. You remember the young girl who was abducted right off the street corner?"

Patricia accepted the case when her husband requested her assistance. The girl's mother had moved her so deeply that she was compelled to dig deeper. But just as Patricia had tied it to other missing persons cases with a similar MO, communication came from DC to drop the investigation. She ignored the order and continued to work the case on her off time, counting herself fortunate that this did not inhibit her promotion.

"How about we focus on your awards ceremony and discuss this later?" He glanced at his wife and caught her fidgeting in the seat.

"I'll hold you to that." She pulled the visor down to check her hair. "Oh look, there it is, finally."

When they arrived at the hotel, a young valet took the keys from her husband. Arm in arm, they walked into the hotel lobby where they were directed to the elevators. They pressed the button and enjoyed the spectacular view of the city through the glass lift to the plaza pool deck—a 45,000-square-foot outdoor area for the party under the stars.

To Patricia's bewilderment, a gauntlet of applauding agents and friends lined the way to her guest of honor position at the main table. Her crimson cheeks flushed at the attention. She let go of her husband's arm only long enough to find her seat as the FBI deputy director motioned to quiet the room.

The guests sat at tables and chairs surrounding fire pits among the brightly lit box trees. The sky had faded to a deep purple accented by the lighting trusses, from which party lights hung across the deck. A large bar sat at the far end of the venue with an enclosed DJ booth framing the stairs that rose to the pool deck.

Approaching the podium, Deputy Director Fairbanks tapped on the mic, drawing a squeal of audio feedback, and then committed to keeping the speech short—it was not the only promise he broke in the evening.

He lauded Patricia for her hard work and dedication, citing an incredible record of successfully closed cases over her lengthy career. Having previously garnered the FBI star and the meritorious achievement awards, Patricia was all smiles and dazzled with sparkling eyes in her moment of triumph, accepting a large crystal plate to commemorate her receiving the FBI's highest honor—the director's award. She acknowledged that without the cooperation of her fellow investigators and team members, she could not stand in front of them all on this occasion. This was 'an award to be celebrated by all'.

Praise for the FBI in general was the next order of business for the deputy director.

"Our team has seen a lot of challenges in the past few years. In the face of our most recent scandal, the DOJ rose to the call, and as a result, the director of the FBI may be removed from service. I'm not here to provide my feelings on the judgement but to illustrate and remind you all that the pressure and the spotlight are uniquely focused on our entire organization."

Patricia recalled the shock waves that rumbled through the department. She had felt the personal burden of rebuilding trust with an untrusting nation in the midst of an election-year scandal, and assumed that was the main reason the press had been allowed to attend the festivities.

"We gather this evening to celebrate the success of one of our own." He paused while the group applauded lightly. "But the truth is, the L.A. office has successfully handled more cases in the past 10 years than any other branch. I've spent much time here and can attest to the fact that these are some of the hardest working agents in our employ…"

Patricia's husband, Brad, noticed the deputy director seemed to be speaking to the press more than the agents. "He's grandstanding." He removed a toothpick from his mouth and spoke under his breath to his wife. "I didn't realize the FBI was so political."

"It's a government agency, BB, of course it's political. You realize he's next in line should the director be removed." A smirk took over her mouth.

"If that's the case, he's lost my vote."

"You don't get to vote on that, silly." She shushed her husband.

"…at a time when we needed to rebuild the public's confidence in law enforcement and perhaps in government on the whole, the FBI responded in exemplary fashion. And it is through the hard work and dedication of agents like yourselves," he swept his arm across the crowd. "And Patricia Barnes that we are able to restore trust in our system."

Brad was happy that the deputy director returned the focus to Patricia and the lengthy speech was coming to an end. Until Fairbanks found occasion to bore the gathering with talk about his own career and rise through the bureau. He concluded with an 'I'll always have your back' statement as a binding mechanism.

"I'm glad that's finally over. I shudder to think what the long version would've been like." He chuckled.

Patricia kissed him on the cheek and whispered, "Let's not make a scene and we may be able to get out of here with some time for ourselves."

What ensued was a night of socializing and drinking. The director had cut the open bar off early—the second broken promise of the night. When it was over and all the congratulations had been given, Patricia felt she should have been exhausted, but she wasn't. She told her husband she wanted time to wind down.

As they stepped out of the lobby, Patricia cut in front of her husband and took the keys from the valet. He asked them where they were headed and then warned them that the 10 freeway was closed due to construction. That left them with the 110 to the 105 to navigate to their Santa Monica home, or a drive through the busy streets of Hollywood.

"So much for some time to ourselves," Brad whistled lightly. "First that boring speech, and now this."

The valet suggested the ride up the coast might be nicer and would also avoid most of the traffic signals.

"Oh, that sounds so much more enjoyable, love. I need to relax, and you know how I love the drive along the ocean." She bent into a coy smile.

"Yes, dear, but you've had a few cocktails and I think it would be better if I drove this time. You can still enjoy the night sky and revel in your achievement." Brad convinced her otherwise with a raised eyebrow and a firm look of disapproval.

She leveled the playing field with a sexy twist that found her brushing against him on her way past, handing him the keys.

"You're right." She smiled. "But I must warn you, I'm feeling a little amorous."

Brad noticed a surge of blood below his beltline. "Then, by all means, let's get moving."

"Thanks for the advice, young man, you've earned it." He handed the valet a crisp 20-dollar bill, and they were on their way.

In less than 30 minutes, they cruised through the south bay curve and were soon eyeing palm trees and catching the light from the moon's reflection on the ocean. They eased by Patrick's Roadhouse and then Will Roger's Beach Park, headed to Las Pulgas Canyon, where they would make the turn for home.

As the Rover pulled to the stop light at Temescal Canyon, she turned toward her husband and rubbed his lap. "I want you tonight, Bradford, and I will take you."

He leaned over and kissed her, smiling. She was the only person he allowed to call him by his full name.

"But when we're done, remind me to talk to you about the case you gave me." She reclined her seat a little. "You remember, I talked about it earlier. The young girl, Reagan?"

"Why, have you found new information?" Brad checked the rearview mirror when the car behind flashed his headlights.

"You gave us the camera footage on the car that she got into."

"Yeah, the driver was dressed as a priest, right?" He drummed his fingers on the steering wheel impatiently, waiting for the signal to change.

"Right. Unfortunately, none of the footage was usable for facial recognition. The vehicle was stolen and wiped clean, not even a trace of evidence…no prints or hair to run in a DNA test."

"That's why we passed it to you." His gaze drifted to the mirror again.

"I was able to find other cases and cross-referenced them. Same MO, different locations all on or near the coast but never the same city twice."

"Were you able to get clean photos or evidence?" Headlights flashed again and the car inched closer.

"No, but I took all the data and triangulated the locations…" She paused and looked over her shoulder, hearing tires screech.

The twitchy driver tapped his horn and then sped past on his left. Brad eyed the rude man and flipped him off as he went by. He was focusing on what Patricia had said before easing his foot off the brake pedal to proceed through the intersection.

He didn't even have time to catch it in his periphery, but a huge utility dump truck was barreling down Temescal Canyon right at them. It came so suddenly that he only had a moment to react before it slammed into them.

The collision was tremendous, flipping their expensive SUV over and pushing it across the oncoming lanes. The force of the impact threw their bodies around the interior like rag dolls. When he regained consciousness, the inside of the car was still swirling white with dust from the safety airbags. Glass shards from the shattered windshield were everywhere. Disoriented, Brad realized that the vehicle was on its side, with Patricia held in place above him by her seat belt. The warmth of her blood panicked him as it trickled from her forehead and ears onto his face.

Her eyes were open but unseeing. He could hear the faint gurgling of blood in her breathing. Having seen more than his share of accidents, he knew it was bad and needed to keep her talking until help arrived. He reached up to touch her, but the sharp pain in his shoulder told him it was dislocated. With his left arm, he could get to the horn and honked, trying to get her attention.

She shook into consciousness. "What the heck?"

"We've been hit, Pat. It's bad, but it's going to be okay. You need to keep talking to me. Tell me, baby, what was your favorite part of the party?" He tried to keep her awake.

She tried to talk again, and some blood, thick with mucous, spilled out of her mouth. "It's hard to breathe."

"I know, babe, but you have to keep talking. I need you to focus and keep talking."

"Brad, I'm so cold, so tired."

"No, Pat. No." He almost screamed. "Fight, fight harder than you've ever fought."

"I wish we'd had kids. I know I shouldn't, but I do."

"They would've been brilliant kids, baby." He desperately wanted to reach out to touch her.

"This world can be so ugly, though."

"We've helped, Pat, and you'll continue to help once we get you out of here and into a hospital."

She coughed and her head drooped. Long strands of her auburn hair hung across her face, wet with blood and wiper fluid that had exploded into the interior with the hit.

He honked the horn again and she was back.

"Brad, I wanted to tell you…"

"I know, baby, I love you too. It's going to be alright, just hang on, help is coming. Can you hear the sirens? They're almost here."

"Honey, I can't move. I can't feel anything."

"Stay with me, Pat, just keep talking."

"I needed to tell you…I was going to tell you tonight…" She paused.

"What, Pat? What were you going to tell me?"

"That case, the girl…Reagan. The FBI instructed me to close it."

"It was a dead end, Pat. That's why I gave it to you. Just in case there was something we missed. You had more tools than we did."

"They've never asked me to close a case that wasn't solved."

"It's okay. We'll talk to them, right? Once you've healed, we'll talk to them." He just wanted to keep her talking.

"Brad? I can't see anything." More blood and her breathing became more erratic. "Not…much…time…"

The sirens were now blaring. They were pulling up to the scene. Voices—loud, sharp—and the sound of boots hitting the pavement were now audible.

"They are here, baby. You'll be out of here in a minute and on the way to the hospital. It's going to be okay." He was trying to convince her to hang on.

"Brad, the girl...the case...to get the...point." Her head twitched back and forth. The gurgling was heavy. She was drowning in her own blood.

"No, Pat. NO!" She lost consciousness again. He screamed and honked the horn as the fire crew reached the vehicle. "Get her! GET HER OUT! NOW!"

She lifted her head slightly and turned towards his voice and mouthed, *I love you.*

CHAPTER 1

A biting wind swept over the dark, foreboding ocean, across the parking area, and found its way into the rear of the ambulance, chilling old Doc Nichols. The wet mist argued with the breeze, nipping at him like an angry Chihuahua. Above, the shrill cry of scavenging birds broke the morbid silence.

A thin cloth blanket draped over slumping shoulders was his lone defense against the cold. Deep, labored breathing fogged an oxygen mask whose elastic rubber straps sent his matted gray hair askew. It was late in the morning now and he had just endured a battering of questions that sapped what limited energy he had left, rendering him exhausted.

Hunched forward and motionless, he rested on the gurney, gazing out of the open back doors of the emergency vehicle. Through heavily lidded, bloodshot eyes, he monitored the parade of police activity in the otherwise empty beach parking lot. A few droplets of water clung to his chin from the last sip of a plastic bottle he cradled in feeble, quivering hands.

Standing in a patchy fog about a hundred feet away were the two detectives who had interrogated him intensely. They appeared as shadows in the early morning light—the dawn still hidden by the coastal mountains.

After ducking under the caution tape, they had stopped near the only civilian vehicle in the parking lot—his own Silver Mercedes C500. Nichols could see that both were preoccupied with note-taking devices. They looked up only occasionally to survey the gory crime scene, taking in diverse angles, trying to piece together the evidence with the doc's account of events.

The younger of the two men sported the typical cop mustache and wore aviator sunglasses. He looked as if he'd stepped right out of a prime-time police series. "I'm worried about the doc."

The second detective was clearly the veteran of the team.

"He's had a heckuva run that old guy," said the seasoned Bradford Barnes, chewing on a toothpick as he proceeded to the front of the car to get a better look. He considered the familiar itching in his fingers and on his lips—the nagging tingle reminding him of where the cigarette should be.

Blood smudged the hood of the sedan on the driver's side. A pool of thick red, gooey fluid pooled on the asphalt as it dripped from the left front fender. A thin white sheet of plastic covered a lifeless body 15 feet away, hiding the sight from a small crowd gathering at the east end of the parking area.

The Lookie Loos, nothing better to do, he thought. *Can't blame them, death always brings interest. Murder asks questions that beg for answers.*

Twenty years on the force had seen Barnes try to quit smoking more times than he cared to admit. Now, standing in the middle of another homicide scene, the pressure was building again. Two dead bodies—a young man, thirties, almost a ghostly white-blue color to his skin, head drawn back, mouth wide open gasping for air that wouldn't come. His dark red eyelids framed open eyes staring into nowhere in the direction of the second man on the other side of the sandy bluffs.

He bit down and crushed the small wooden sliver between his teeth before spitting it into the street. "Useless piece of shit," he cursed as he put his heel to it and ground it into the weather-beaten slurry. Then, with lips pressed tightly together and a heavy sigh of resignation, he begrudgingly reached into his coat pocket and pulled out a fresh surrogate. He sucked it securely between his teeth, relentless with yearning.

"A heckuva run indeed," repeated his partner.

At six foot two inches tall, he was the same height as his senior cohort, but that is where the comparisons ended. Following a 48-month stint in Iraq, Colton Noble had been with the department for a tick over eight years and made detective only a handful of months prior. A local boy, he was a stickler for detail and did everything by the book. He was as smart as he was handsome and as handsome as he was fit.

He'd surely have been promoted to detective sooner, but in a small beach town like Rocky Point, opportunities were limited. Retirement typically presented new openings, though there was the occasional firing or, even worse, the death of a fellow officer.

Through lips that barely moved on a hard, squared jaw, he continued, "Just a few months ago, the doc's wife turns up dead and then he stumbles into this mess, sheesh."

Barnes reached under his blue sport coat and readjusted his shoulder holster. "That's right, I remember you talking about that. Grimes was working that case, wasn't he?"

"It was his last before he…well, you know," Noble answered, almost choking on the words that hung in the sullen moment.

After alleviating the pinch of the holster's leather straps, Barnes shrugged his shoulders, loosening his coat. "Man, that had to have been a tough situation. You guys all being so close, it must've rocked the department." He scribbled something on his notepad.

"Hard to put into words, Brad. The guy was here 37 years." Noble turned his head slightly, realigning his neck. "He was a mentor and a confidant to almost everyone in the department. Shoot, he was the department."

"And you had to be the one to find him, huh?" Barnes uttered in his most consoling tone.

"It might have destroyed some of the others," Colt stiffened, hoping for some warmth as a slight orange glow hinted from the east. "Better it was me, I suppose."

"I didn't know him long, met him only once at a council meeting when I first got here. His reputation for great instincts and being thorough made him seem like a real good cop."

Noble refocused his gaze out toward the ocean as a wave broke on the shoreline, rumbling across the cove. "As good a cop as they come." His shoulders heaved.

"Hey, kid, I've been doing this awhile now too, you realize?" Barnes mentioned.

"Oh, I uh…I wasn't comparing or anything, I was just saying that…" Noble stammered.

Barnes cut him off with a quick chuckle. "'Colt', come on, I was kidding. I've gotta do something to break the tension here, or I'll be back puffing on the coffin nails in no time."

Noble managed a little smirk. "Right, of course. It's just…he helped me a lot, you know?"

Barnes nervously tapped his pencil on his pad. "I get it, kid. Maybe that was bad timing on my part. Why don't we just get back to it, huh?"

Colt rubbed a calloused hand across his face, temporarily erasing the stinging memory.

"Sure thing. You wanna take it from the beginning again?"

CHAPTER 2

How grand the beauty storms can bring.

If there was ever a moment to bask in triumph, this may have been it. Confident and comfortable, William Winslow Walker Jr. sat behind the desk in his lavishly decorated office in the historic government estate. The incumbent democratic nominee had just defended his senatorial seat.

A light dusting of snow blanketed the lawn and hedges in the courtyard of the Hampton House, waiting for the Connecticut sun to breach the clouds and melt it away. The flutter of blackbird wings whished in the grey, still morning. Most of the state's appointed and elected officials telecommuted given the inclement weather, but there were a few who braved the conditions because this was a special day.

Propelled by his position on civil rights, he was back on familiar turf. The results evinced that his constituents felt comfortable with his history and impeccable reputation. It had not been a landslide victory, but his re-election was never in question. The senator had gerrymandering and generous campaign contributions to thank for that.

He'd always enjoyed scanning the headlines on his tablet following the voting. Deep brown eyes widened as he reclined in his burgundy high-backed, leather-upholstered chair. The apex of his nose was home to a scowl where thick, overgrown salt and pepper eyebrows angled on a foreboding brow. He tilted a head almost devoid of hair on the top to reduce the glare coming from the window.

With a mouth fixed in a semi-permanent frown and framed by deep wrinkles that cut their way to the jowls on his jawline, his cheeks jittered as he read. His six-foot-one-inch frame that carried over 300 pounds made him an imposing figure, to say the least.

He sneered after taking in the headline on the screen. 'LEGACY LOOMS LARGE,' it read. He recognized the phrase as a double entendre, aimed not only at his family's lineage in the political landscape but also a dig at his physical presence. He made a mental note of the writer's name for future reference.

Martin Bender again, huh? What is this guy's problem? He's been all over me from the first term. Little pissant can't even recognize greatness when he sees it. I step on bigger bugs than this cockroach taking a leak at night.

He set the tablet on the desk, wrestled himself out of his chair, and huffed and puffed his way over to the library stack at the back of the office. Under the counter, he engaged a small, hidden button. While waiting, he scanned a regal-looking, hand-painted portrait that hung above the sink.

An entire automated bar was slow to open and replaced the fake shelves and law books. The senator dropped a couple of ice cubes into a small glass and then filled it halfway with scotch.

He looked up at the portrait and toasted his father, William Walker Sr., before gulping a mouthful of the smooth alcohol. "To the future," he said with a wink. "Another six years of this bullshit to look forward to, I guess," he continued, grumbling under his breath as he labored toward the window. "It's amazing what a small sum of money and a few carefully placed words can do."

He considered his role as a politician much more manipulator than anything else, and he was certain he had mastered this skill. Yet, despite the slight adrenaline rush the victory provided, 'Winslow,' as they knew him in political circles, wasn't overly excited regarding his renewed mandate.

The win would mean a second term spent representing people who he believed had no clue what the genuine issues were. He did not feel this was a valid use of his capabilities. However, the political position he held was particularly useful in establishing his philanthropic ventures, such as his non-profit organization helping battered women and children.

Why can't that reporter focus on the things I've done for this state? he lamented. *What has he ever accomplished? Besides, the people have chosen. As long as the citizens of this state continue to have a stable economy, they won't even care about the issues. What an arcane system.* He smiled.

He held his glass up to the light and checked the level of remaining alcohol. "And where will that cocksucker, Martin Bender, be when this is all over?" He tossed the last of the remnants of scotch down his gullet. "Well, scrounging for his next meal if I have anything to say about it," he ranted out loud as if hearing it gave it more meaning.

A long wooden wand twisted in his hands and the blinds opened. The rotund politician stood at the window, rocking on his heels. Winslow rattled the ice in the empty glass and his free hand found its way into the waistband of his slacks. Surveying the expansive grounds outside, he wondered why he had to maintain this farce. He had cached far more than enough money into his overseas accounts than he'd ever need to live out his ostentatious lifestyle.

But then he heard it...those familiar words ringing in his ears. 'Living as a common man is foolishness,' Senior had bellowed to his oldest son. 'You must seek reverence from the common man. To be revered, you must have power, position, and prestige. To gain those, you must have money, and a lot of it.'

"Here, here." He hoisted the glass over his shoulder in the direction of the portrait, and bored with his courtyard view, returned to the bar to refresh his drink. "Well, I suppose you knew a thing or three," he said, talking at the painting. "I guess six more years won't be so tough. But how you made it through four terms of this circus is beyond me. This is my last term fighting for issues that will never be resolved." He pumped another seven ounces of scotch into his system and set the empty glass on the counter. "Besides, we've got bigger fish to fry, right, Senior?"

After a few more minutes of personal reflection at the bar, the senator plodded back to his desk. He picked up the tablet and continued reading.

'I'm afraid we're just going to see more of the same apathetic approach from the Senator out of Avon,' the article went on.

'In a nation divided over so many issues, his alcoholic binges or recurring absences commonly overshadow the senator's rhetoric on human rights. He has done little to refute the accusations of corruption, spending long afternoons on the golf course with union leaders and contractors. This simple and blatant disregard for his responsibilities should raise the ire of every voter and every citizen of our great state. Not only is Senator Walker unfit for office, but he is also simply unfit, period.'

Walker Jr. pulled a heavy desk drawer open and tossed the tablet in angrily. "Mr. Bender, we are headed on a collision course, you and I." He clenched his jaw and turned his neck, generating a violent snap. A crack so loud, he almost did not hear the knock at his door.

"Yes, come in please."

A very plain-looking middle-aged woman with auburn hair in a bun and dark-rimmed glasses peered around the door.

"I'm sorry to bother you, Senator, but there is a call waiting for you on line one. I tried to take a message. However, the party was very adamant about speaking with you directly."

"Oh, that's alright, Gwen," he responded with a dismissive wave. "I'll take the call. Did they mention what this is regarding? It wasn't Martin Bender, was it?" He laughed.

"I'm sorry, sir, I didn't get the name," she apologized.

"Never mind, Gwen." He smiled. "It's not important. Thanks for making me aware."

She backed out of the room quietly, leaving the door open a crack.

The senator looked at the red light blinking on the phone and had thoughts about just clicking it off. But since it was a day of celebration, he figured it might be of a congratulatory nature—likely one of his democratic compatriots—and picked up the receiver.

"Senator Walker, how can I serve you?" he answered in his most contrived politicians speak.

"Senator William Winslow Walker Jr.?" the gruff voice asked.

"The very same," he bellowed. "Now, what can I do for you today?"

There was a brief pause and a sigh. "Senator, this is 'Gridlock,' and we have a problem."

"Hold on," the senator ordered. He popped up out of his chair and rushed to the office door, shuffling without even bending at the knee. He closed it with a slam.

Gwen nearly jumped out of her skin at her desk.

"You were most certainly informed never to contact me at the office!" he barked. "Those were strict orders. You know the rules. Your negligent actions could compromise everything." The senator was now fuming into the phone. "Why on earth didn't you use proper protocol?"

"Senator, we followed protocol but you did not respond, and the nature of the call was critical."

"Why didn't you call the secure line?" he asked, looking around the office for his cell phone. "Shit!"

"Sir, we tried that line. Sir, I'm sorry to inform you but—" The caller paused again. "Sir, the 'bottom' has dropped out."

"What?" the senator asked in disbelief as a wave of terror tore through his body and he shivered as though an icy breeze had blown in. "Is this some kind of joke? You'd darn well better have your facts straight. That can't be. That can't possibly be."

"Senator, the 'bottom' has dropped out." There was a click and the line went dead.

CHAPTER 3

As if completely weightless, she was floating on a cloud—warm, soft, fuzzy…yes, everything seemed fuzzy.

She could hear things, voices…distant but there. More like mumblings or murmurs that she couldn't quite make out. But more than one person she thought, sure.

There was the occasional sound of feet shuffling to and from. Reagan knew she should have felt terrified, but instead, she was just fuzzy…warm and fuzzy.

The *where am I* and *how did I get here* questions fell to the wayside because she just didn't have the focus to trace backwards. She felt confused, her memory was foggy…her mind sluggish. A thought broke through—a lucid moment. She flashed on bits and pieces of things, but nothing seemed clear. A fight with a woman, yelling, screaming…physical. Her mom?

No, the man in the smock said her mom was gone. They were all gone. That's why she was here, she'd had a breakdown of sorts, a schism, he'd said. They were bringing her back slowly with medication and psychotherapy. She searched her memory.

Did I hurt my mom? What happened? Why can't I think clearly, why can't I remember? Her frustration was building, her thoughts were coming quicker. She grabbed her hair and moaned. She felt the plastic hose attached to her arm brush against her and the restraints across her torso. *Why am I tied up? Why is my room always dark?* "Someone help me!" she screamed.

The shuffling of feet again…a blast of light. The smock was there, safety mask across his face…but the eyes, dark, devoid of emotion staring back at her. Fear was building.

"This'll only take a second, sweet thing," he soothed. Seconds later, the bag had been switched and he held her hand, squeezing.

The anger passed but the fear had intensified. This didn't feel right. She was scared…had questions but couldn't formulate them into words. The warm sensation was coursing through her body again.

"Roll it," the smock said as he left the room and the darkness cascaded over her again.

Speakers crackled and the audio began.

"This is your new life. Your old life is gone." Each time, another sentence was added, building on the first. "This is your new life. Your old life is gone. Your new life is better…"

She tried to lift her head and look around, but in the stillness of the pitch-black room, she found only confusion before drifting into unconsciousness again.

Warm.

Fuzzy.

Peaceful.

CHAPTER 4

"Okay, from the beginning again, huh?" Barnes opened his notepad and motioned toward the ambulance.

"We've got two dead bodies, both males, mid-thirties. One up here on the parking lot by the doc's car and the other over the bluff. Doc says they were fighting, I'm trying to figure out how they ended up so far apart if they were fighting."

"Maybe the guy over the bluff was fleeing the scene?"

"Okay, let's try to put this together." Barnes paused. "Doc up there says he's headed down to the beach for some 'private' time, right?"

"Yeah," a distracted Noble moved to where Barnes was standing by the Mercedes. "That's an awful lot of blood." He snapped a photo of the hood with his tablet. "Almost looks like too much for one guy. Big dent there on the hood. You think he made that just by leaning on it?"

"Doc said the guy was in extreme pain," Barnes said, moving around to the open driver's side door. "Maybe he hit it or something, I don't know." Looking around the vehicle, he noticed small circles painted on the pavement, marked with small paper tents identifying beer cans and a baseball cap and other items. He gathered his slacks at the knee and crouched down near evidence tent number three.

He attempted to lift a square wooden object off of the asphalt with his pencil. It was unsuccessful, so he retrieved a latex glove from his left coat pocket and blew into the protective cover, inflating it to make it easier to slip on. He then flipped the object over.

A couple of small shards of glass fell off of the frame and clinked to the street. The remaining pieces covered a now slightly distorted image.

Colton cocked his head and moved in behind his kneeling partner. Peering over his shoulder, he recognized the girl in the photo. "That's Corrina, the doc's dead wife we were talking about earlier."

The older detective thought immediately back to the accident that took his beloved Patricia months earlier. The feelings of helplessness returned, and overcome with guilt, he wondered what the doc had faced with the loss of his young wife. He knew he would never be whole again and empathized with the old physician. Barnes returned the frame to the ground and stood up straight, pulling the glove off of his hand.

"Yeah, I recognize her from the case photo. She looks so young." Without turning away completely, he tilted his head in Noble's direction. "Hey, what did Grimes determine as the cause of death in the case of Doc's wife, anyway? Was he able to finish the investigation, before he uh…"

Colt spat toward the ambulance and wiped at his chin. "Suicide."

"So, he finished the investigation, then?" Barnes was still fixated on the photo.

"Filed it myself, you know after…" Colt responded.

Barnes just couldn't seem to look away from the picture. A crack ran lengthwise on the remaining piece of glass still in the frame, splitting her image in half.

"Shame," he commented.

"Yeah, a gorgeous girl. Can't be much more than mid-thirties," Colt remarked. "Never could understand how someone who seemed to have it all would just throw it away so easily."

The elder detective ran his hand through a tuft of oddly thick hair that a sudden gust of wind had displaced. He couldn't shake the feeling of déjà vu that the girl's image ignited.

"I'm certain that determining to check out is not as easy as you think. In my experience, a person has to be in a horrible place to move to that decision."

Colt rocked back a bit and placed both hands in the pockets of his pleated, pinstriped slacks. "Well, I don't know the entire backstory. That may be true. But she sure appeared to have a glorious life."

"How's that?" asked Barnes. "We only see things from the outside. We don't always know what goes on behind closed doors."

Colton took a hand from his pocket and ran it across his nostrils. "I'm just thinking…big house, big pool, big car, and plenty of money to travel or do what she wanted. And a guy that obviously loved her dearly."

"Loved her dearly?" questioned Barnes. "And what led you to that conclusion? Am I missing something, do you know the doc well?"

"Don't have to know him to know that." Colt reached behind his back, into the waistband of his slacks, and pulled out his tablet. He powered the screen on and started tapping at it frantically. "Now, give me a second to find the right clip. I think you may have stepped away for just a second to talk to forensics after asking the question of why he was here so early."

He dragged a finger across the touch screen and then listened as a crystal-clear recording of Doc Nichols played.

A gravelly voice recounted, "Like so many other mornings recently, I'd driven down here before work. I wanted to be as close to Corrina as I could. She loved this place. We used to come here often. I don't recall her ever smiling as much as when she was down there in the sand." The doc paused and his breathing became more pronounced. "I must've taken about a million pictures of her. She would be wearing some kind of light sun dress with a great big woven hat and those big bug-eye type sunglasses. Reminded me of an old movie starlet."

It was almost like he was watching a film the way he told it, Barnes thought.

"She'd drag me down to the water's edge and splash at me, trying to get me to chase her, I think. She made everything fun, made me feel young and alive. Then she would spin in circles until she got dizzy and fell. To dry her toes off, she would wriggle them deep into the sand just like a little kid, so playful. We'd watch the sun rise over the mountains, her leaning into it as if she could somehow siphon its warmth directly. She loved it here. And I loved her here."

Noble tapped the screen again and the file stopped playing. "You see, the way I figure it, the doc is down here reliving the memories of his dead wife and he's got the picture in his lap; soaking it all in when he drifts off." The younger detective continued quietly for effect, "Then WHAM!" he yelled, clapping his hands, startling Barnes. "This guy, Walker, hits the hood and wakes him up from a dead sleep. The doc gets out to help him before he even remembers the picture is in his lap. And that's how the photo ends up here."

"I can do without the theatrics, kid," Barnes said, pocketing his notepad, the ravages of time becoming more evident in his old ways. "But that's a reasonable conclusion."

Barnes looked down at the trail of blood and followed it leading away from the Mercedes. "This guy must've been running on empty," he said to Noble, who had quickly tucked in behind him.

"Doc said that's likely what killed him…the loss of blood, I mean. He said he couldn't stop the bleeding, tried wrapping him with those bandages we saw around his midsection." Noble was about to pull the pad out of his waistband again.

"I get it, kid. We don't need the electronics light show this time," Barnes grumbled, retrieving his paper notepad. He held it up over his shoulder without looking back. "I was there. I heard it. I took notes myself and I don't need to have it played back for me."

"You got eyes in the back of your head or something?" Noble released his grip on the tablet.

Barnes slowed. "Yeah, you might want to remember that, kid. I see everything." He chuckled.

"Boo," Noble waxed sarcastic fear. "Doc said that if this guy had just stayed by the car, he'd probably still be alive, or at least would've had a better chance."

"All of this extra physical exertion just drained him, I suppose." Barnes scratched at his temple. "But why this guy is trying to crawl away from the car in the first place is confusing to me. I mean, was he scared of the doc for some reason?"

Noble folded his arms across his hardened chest. "Survival mechanism, maybe?" He turned from the spot where Walker had crawled and glanced toward the beach. "If the doc's story holds true, then Walker's attacker goes over the bluff there after stabbing him. That's when the doc heard the other guy scream out for help, right?"

"Okay," Barnes accepted.

"Then, Walker here," Noble pointed back to the light post where the body was covered by a plastic sheet. "Walker here tells the doc this other guy is dangerously deranged. He warned and begged the doc not to go and help him, but the he goes over the bluff, anyway." Noble gathered his thoughts for an instant. "Maybe the doc is gone so long that Walker thinks the assailant killed him?"

"Have we found any phones yet? Why didn't anyone call 911 immediately?" Barnes was growing irritated. "One guy is stabbed…another is trying to escape over the sandy bluff? Can we please get the phones and look at the history?"

CHAPTER 5

A young woman in forensics was busily collecting samples from the area around the car. Barnes asked her to stand down for a minute as he got back to the driver's side of the Mercedes. He looked in but didn't see any blood on the seat. He was about to press the unlock mechanism when he noticed traces of blood on the door's armrest.

"Tricia," Barnes called out to the agent. "Can I get some samples here, please?" He pointed to the armrest and ignition. "Thanks, and give me a shout when you're done."

The agent nodded understandingly.

Noble looked around and, pointing toward the sky, said, "We should probably see if these cameras on the light posts caught anything too."

"Good call, kid," Barnes offered. "It's foggy but maybe we will get a break. Can you get someone on it?"

Noble hustled off toward one of the patrol units and instructed an officer to hunt for a surveillance office.

When he returned, Barnes was still at the front of the car but was now looking out at the ocean. "You know," he said pensively, surveying the horizon. "I came out here thinking that I could get away from this stuff, that I'd be coming to a place where the pace was a little bit slower and the people were a little friendlier. I guess it doesn't really matter where you are, bad people are everywhere."

"Yeah, Brad?" Noble waited, expecting more.

Barnes waved his arm in the direction of the beach. "How could a place this beautiful be anything less than a peaceful haven?"

"Sometimes bad just finds a way in." Colt patted his partner's back. "It's our job to snuff it out. Shoot, Brad, if it was always peaceful, they wouldn't need us here. You'd still be back in L.A. choking away at a two-pack-a-day habit."

From where he stood, Barnes could take in the whole beach. He looked to the south and followed the trail as it wound its way from the end of the parking lot to the old lighthouse on the cliff that overlooked the sharp, craggy rocks the town had been named after. A historical landmark, the 40-foot beacon appeared to be in as good a condition as when it was first constructed.

The beach itself was relatively secluded and spanned only a little over a quarter of a mile between the two points, from the lighthouse to the cliffs on the north. Most of it remained hidden by sandy bluffs that eventually gave way to a beautiful boardwalk, but once crested, the beauty was inspiring.

"How old is that thing?" Barnes asked, turning towards the lighthouse.

"Been here since 1901." Noble rubbed at the back of his neck.

"Anybody still live there that might have seen something?" Barnes quizzed.

Noble snickered. "It's the 21st century, Brad. Not many people left with any appreciation for the old way of doing things. Everything is automated now. It was converted to timers years ago. Just a maintenance crew every so often now."

"Converted, huh?" Barnes saw an opening. "Probably by a bunch of 'tablet tappers', I'm guessing."

Noble shook his head. "The world keeps spinning, Brad. Can't stop it."

"I guess," Barnes accepted. "The trail is still there though, and it looks well-traveled."

"Lighthouses are big tourist attractions these days. At least a dozen times a year, the town sponsors tours for visitors. They've been considering renovating and turning it into a bed and breakfast." Noble cracked his knuckles. "But mostly just kids up there these days. They come from all over. They find a way through or over the fence, trying to get to the upper deck so they can party. We've had a few jumpers over the years, too."

"Jumpers, huh?" Barnes assessed the distance to the rocks below to be at least 100 feet. "I wouldn't even fly a kite over that drop."

Noble looked perplexed. "You scared of heights, Brad?"

"No, not so much scared as just have a healthy respect for," Barnes lied.

Noble squinted at the lighthouse. "Well, they rebuilt the fence not too long ago and it's been pretty quiet out there recently. The last jumper happened just a few months before you got here. Weird too, they always end up in the same place. Every single one of them. The tide comes in, picks 'em up, and deposits them right in the center of the beach."

"How do you know they jumped?" Barnes raised his collar as a brisk wind coming in off the ocean began to pick up.

"Well," Noble pursed his lips. "Routine deductions, I suppose. There are broken bones, wounds consistent with blunt force trauma, and gouges from the rocks while the tide scrapes them away." He paused. "Oh, and suicide notes, of course."

Barnes gave his partner a playful shove. "You can be such a prick sometimes."

Rocking slightly off balance, Noble smiled. "Yeah, the notes do help a little."

"Speaking of suicide notes," Barnes turned toward Colt. "Did Doc's wife leave a note?"

"Nope, I remember Grimes asking the doc about reasons she might've done it," Noble responded. "Either way, she checked out, right?"

"No note usually means it was an accident or a snap decision." Barnes' face got very serious. "Often, people leave notes to try and lay blame or make someone else feel bad. They try to justify their actions. Typically, folks who do it on the fly are either in so much pain that they can't go on or are punishing themselves."

"They teach that down there in L.A., do they?" Noble coughed.

"No, you learn that with experience. It's not bulletproofed, of course, but there's something to it," Barnes said, stepping back towards the car just in time to see Eugene and the coroner team skipping the bluff to get to the second body, ready to examine it before carting it into the wagon.

"Speaking of experience," Noble said, pointing to the second of the two homicide scenes. "What do you make of all this out here?"

"Too early to tell at this point," Barnes answered. "But we'd better get over there and finish this thing. It's already been a long day."

"No arguing that."

Barnes shot a look toward the police tape at the entrance to the parking lot. As he did, he picked up a tall guy in an all-black suit and dark glasses on his cellular, not blending in very well. "We need to send someone up there to move those folks offsite. We could be here for a while yet."

"No problem," Noble turned and headed out. "I'm on it."

The crowd, which had gathered at the head of the parking lot throughout the course of the morning, had grown substantially. Curious onlookers were becoming impatient for information and beachgoers were eager to get to the sand.

"Hey, kid," Barnes yelled out. "Find out who the suit is and who he's with. Put some pressure on him. We don't need any press until we're ready."

"Got it."

CHAPTER 6

Colton made it back over the bluff just as Barnes was pocketing his notepad.

"Alright, Barnsie, the nosy crazies have been dispersed."

"Great, maybe we can keep a lid on this a bit longer before it hits the big media." Barnes thanked his partner.

"Good luck with that," Colton laughed.

"Any word on the suit? Were you able to find out who he was with and get him to stay tight-lipped?" Barnes cursed the sand getting in his shoes.

"Sorry, bud." Colton looked at his partner. "No suit anywhere in sight. You wearing your contact lenses? Maybe the weather is getting to you?"

"I don't need them and the weather is fine," he barked back.

Noble feigned a cower. "Right, then, everything is fine."

"Ah, never mind," Barnes dismissed the nonsense. "Can we get back to work?"

"I thought you needed some levity or you'd be back to puffing 'coffin nails'?

Barnes immediately reached into his coat pocket for another toothpick.

"Better?" Noble smiled.

"Yeah, a little, I guess." Barnes sucked in air between his teeth. "Alright, Doc claims to have found the second guy on the back side of this bluff...nose was twisted, blood everywhere."

Barnes knelt and looked over the body of the second man—an athletically fit, 30 to 40-year-old black male.

"What are you looking for?" Noble watched.

"Well, broken nose, that much is obvious, and a knife wound in the chest according to Eugene. I'm no expert, but it doesn't appear deep enough to have caused any significant damage...not much blood. I'm perplexed, though. Doc says this guy was in cardiac arrest. Built like this?"

"Maybe the knife got deep enough? Or maybe there were drugs involved, cocaine, meth, fentanyl?" Noble suggested.

"Yeah, we'll have to get a toxicology report and see what we might have missed, what these guys may have on them. We're going to need the coroner to work fast on this one." Barnes shrugged in his sport coat.

"Eugene is the best. He'll get us what we need, quickly."

"He's got bloody handprints all over him," Barnes commented. "Guess that's from the doc trying compression. He said he couldn't generate enough strength to make a difference."

"Okay, so Nichols does what he can with the first guy, crude stitches and wrapped him tight to try and stem some of the bleeding," Noble described. "Doc said before he went over the bluff, Walker told him about this guy on the beach here, was pissed off at him over a girl or something?"

Barnes smiled. "Holding his hand in the air, he let a plastic bag unroll, grasping the top. That checks out. We found this on him." Inside the bag was the matchbox with a bright red logo in the shape of a mark left by lipstick after a kiss.

"Lovergirls, huh?" said the partner. "Ever been there?"

"I've been here about five weeks. Haven't had time to go dancing yet." The sarcasm spilled over.

"Not the kind of place you'd go dancing, Brad. What a frigging dive!" hissed Colton.

"You know it, huh?" Barnes' eyes caught his young partner's.

"Not like that, 'Detective Judgy'. It's on the outer edge of our precinct. Strip clubs can generate a lot of activity."

"Well, a fight over a girl seems to make sense then, I guess." Barnes took off a shoe and poured out some sand.

"Good thing the doc was here to at least help us piece this together, we'd have been chasing clues out here for days in this chaos," Noble surmised.

Barnes ran a hand through his dense hair. "Don't matter, this place is a DNA nightmare. Sand everywhere mixed with blood and no way to get any footprints, and who knows what's buried under all of this? They'll be gathering and sifting all afternoon."

"What are we looking for? The doc is the only witness. I mean, of course we'll check it out, but it seems pretty straightforward." Noble shrugged.

"Grimes teach you anything?" an annoyed Barnes asked. "Still, the doc's story seems to make some sense."

"I tell ya, the guy comes down here to try and dredge up some peaceful memories and wow, he gets hit with the hammer again," Colton lamented.

"Yeah, you can see it in his face." Barnes looked down at the sand. "This really took a lot out of him."

"You know, Doc here set my kid's broken leg a few years back after that car accident. A lot of folks said he'd never walk right again, but Doc did a good job," Noble mentioned.

"He's got a long history of helping folks out around here, I understand," said Barnes while placing the evidence baggie back in his trench coat pocket. "I remember Grimes talking about him when he was working the wife's case. To hear him tell it, this doc was almost a saint or something. Worked in the clinic for free, donations to charities, second chance foundation chairman, and always took the real tough cases down at the hospital."

"He and Grimes were friends, and yeah, Doc's got quite a reputation," Noble stated matter-of-factly. "You could see that in the outpouring of community when Corrina passed. Old Doc got a lot of support."

Barnes flashed to a memory of his wife's funeral. Big crowd, family, friends, and every agent from her field office. Even Deputy Director Fairbanks was there offering condolences. *"If there's anything you need, Brad, we're here. Just pick up a phone,"* he'd said.

But he was still so angry that he'd missed the opportunity to thank them all. He was living almost exclusively in his head at the time. It was difficult, and realizing that, he knew the doc was in a tough place.

"Well, I guess this all kinda fits together then." Barnes pulled his pad out, almost resigning to the conclusion. "Here he is again trying to do the right thing."

"To hear him talk about how he tried to help these guys but wound up holding each of their hands as they passed," said his partner. "This guy deserves a frigging medal or something."

"No kiddin'. Like we said, a heckuva run indeed."

"I'll tell ya what," Nobles added. "Old Doc isn't on the scene to fill in the blanks for us and we might be looking for a third guy."

Detective Barnes looked up over his pad at his partner with penetrating grey eyes. He closed the small notebook, tapping it rapidly with his stubby pencil, and glanced up toward the ambulance. "Yeah, what a break for us."

CHAPTER 7

"…gone. Your new life is better. You're getting stronger every day. Strong enough to make someone happy…"

The audio kept playing, over and over. She hated it. *Where is the smock?* she wondered. *When will I get out of here?*

The medication was wearing off and she became more coherent, but in the dark of the room, she couldn't see anything. It was confusing. *If I'm getting help, why am I locked away? Do they think I'm dangerous?* she wondered.

The door opened. She saw the silhouette of a huge form squeeze in. He had a tray in his hands…the aroma was strong…food! She instantly realized she was starving.

"Are you ready to eat, Rachel?" he whispered. "It's time to refresh your medicine…"

"Why are you calling me Rachel? I know that is not my name. My name is Reagan. Where is my doctor…"

"Let's not do this again. You do want to eat, don't you?" the voice in the dark soothed empathetically, then continued in a monotone. "This is your new life. Your old life is gone. Your name is Rachel, and if you want food, you'll answer to your new name. This is your new life. Your old life is gone. Your new life will be better."

"Where's my doctor!" she tried to yell but did not have the energy. Her body needed more than the IV was providing. Her dry lips were beginning to crack, her hair felt oily and dirty, her skin itched, and she realized she was scratching at herself.

"You have a few minutes, Rachel, before I change the bag. You still have a long way to go in your recovery, and if you keep fighting, you will make it worse. I suggest that you utilize this opportunity to take some nourishment." The voice was curt this time and he moved to the side of her bed, setting the tray down.

The smell of food had become overwhelming to her…meat, maybe even steak, gravy…possibly mashed potatoes. She was so hungry, so confused, and so sick and tired of the audio that played over and over, even while she slept. *Maybe if I answer to Rachel, this will all come to a stop,* she thought.

"Now then, have you thought this through?" The voice was closer. "Are you ready to eat, or should I take the food away, Rachel?"

"If Rachel eats, will you turn the lights on so I can see?"

"Very promising dear. Welcome, Rachel. Your new life will be better." He smiled under the mask and the wrinkle lines at the sides of his eyes folded. "I can turn on some soft light while you eat." The voice had made its way behind her after he placed the tray onto her stomach.

She felt the bed move and was inclined to a more prone position. A very dim light fell over the space from behind her, just enough to make out the confines of the small room. She could see a counter with cabinets on the wall, a first aid kit, and a hand purifier across from her.

"Where am I?" She heard him fidgeting with the IV bag.

"You're in your new life, Rachel." It sounded like a hiss. "There's a plastic fork on the right of the tray. I urge you to eat fast so you can get strong...strong enough to take your next steps and accept your new life. It's important that you comply, or things could become more difficult."

She didn't waste any time and quickly devoured every morsel on the plate. She did not want it to be taken away.

The man had finished with the bag and made sure the tubing was not tangled. "All done? You must've been very hungry. And, Rachel?"

"Yes?" she answered before realizing she'd responded to her new name.

"You've done well. Your new life is better already, see?"

"Yes, I can see. Can you leave the light on? It's so much nicer like this," she pleaded.

He opened the flow of the IV and spoke. "I suppose you've earned that much today, Rachel. I'll leave the light on for a while."

It was only moments before the warm feeling overcame her and she began to drift off. He gathered the empty food tray and crept out of the room. Seconds later, the audio resumed...

"This is your new life. Your old life is gone. Your new life will be..."

CHAPTER 8

A pensive detective Barnes stared at the foamy head on his drink. *An ice-cold beer has never looked so good,"* he thought. Despite the need to quench a brutal thirst that gripped him following the long investigation at the beach, he resisted the urge to swill the refreshing amber lager in a single gulp.

Instead, he watched with the patience of a monk as an icy trail formed behind a froth of tiny bubbles that had spilled over the side of the frozen mug. He'd become fixated on their sluggish, unfulfilled quest to reach the bar, which reminded him of the handful of cases he left behind since being moved to the missing persons division. Unresolved, they too fell short of the goal.

Unsolved cases beleaguered him. He'd never have left the department and his caseload if not for the unfortunate circumstances that forced his temporary 'vacation'.

His was an efficacious mind, always at work. Even now, he was ruminating on the scene in the parking lot of the beach, the blood on the hood, the two dead bodies, and the picture of the girl. *What was the connection?* he wondered.

Something about the old doctor's story was gnawing at him. It simply would not relinquish its grip. Like a vice, it was relentless and unyielding—almost haunting.

The bell on the front door of the pub he'd stumbled into echoed when a small party of friends rushed in. He snapped back into the moment, glaring toward the commotion at the entrance. Coats were hung and greetings exchanged.

The Crow's Nest was the oldest and most historic pub in Rocky Point, a favorite of locals and visitors alike. As one might expect, the décor was strictly maritime. Most of the interior had been fashioned with the wood and remains of old dry-docked relic boats.

The focal point of the watering hole was a center booth made from the remains of an old crow's nest, salvaged off of a wreck that had been beached on the rocks below the lighthouse more than 150 years prior.

Thick rope hung from the ceiling to the floors in lieu of walls. Old fishing nets, sails, rigging and steering wheels, ripped from their helms, decorated the walls. Amidst the repurposed flotsam hung old photos of Rocky Points' earliest citizens, forever celebrating the town's rich, oceanic heritage.

Time had shown little effect on the venerable structure, but as hard as she fought, the tentacles of modernization had wriggled their way in, and a few big screen televisions littered the center mast for the sporting-minded faithful.

Barnes sat idly in the last seat at the end of a long L-shaped counter, his back to the hallway that led to the bathrooms and the rear entrance. The joint was longer than it was wide but held 90 or so people when full.

The spot that he had chosen provided him with the best view of the front entrance and almost all of the patrons. His reasons were salient. He had a need to be aware of his surroundings at all times. It was a control issue.

He finally relented, taking a few small swallows of the suds that rested patiently in front of him, spinning his glass on the counter between sips. He leaned forward and placed both elbows on the countertop, rubbing at tired eyes.

Did I come here to drink or come here to think? He exhaled a deep, long breath before slogging down the rest of the cold brew that he had been nursing in one gulp. He returned the empty mug to the countertop with a loud thud, designed more to get the bartender's attention than anything else.

"Can I get you another?" the slightly annoyed barkeep asked, rinsing and drying a glass with the rag draped over his shoulder.

"This one's on me," a booming voice came from behind the detective. "And I'll have whatever he's having, Matt. Thanks."

Barnes spun on his barstool and a wide grin broke across his face. "Well, if it isn't the Pride of Rocky Point…how did you know I'd be here, councilman?"

"You know this guy?" laughed the middle-aged drink peddler. "That's a relief. I thought we might've had an escaped mental patient the way he was staring at that drink. Was afraid I was going to have to call on 'ol Maggie Mays' here at some point."

Greasy, long hair shined in the overhead lights as Matt reached down and pulled out a baseball bat he used to keep the peace. He had named her a hybrid of the Rod Stewart song and after the famed Giants slugger, Willie Mays.

"No need for that, Matty, you can put her back. This here's an old friend!" He smiled.

The tall man placed a long arm out and leaned against the bar, squeezing between Barnes and another patron. "Truth is, I didn't know you'd be here, Brad. I came down here for the same reason you probably did, I guess. It's been a tough day for all of us."

"Yeah, I suppose." Barnes tapped at the counter and looked back toward the bartender as he waited on the next lager.

"Not often something like a double homicide goes down in these parts." The councilman winced.

Matt set a couple of tall beers in frozen glasses on the bar in front of them. The councilman placed a 20-dollar bill on the counter. "Keep the change, Matt, and keep 'em coming, will ya?" He turned back to the detective. "You got anything yet, Brad?"

"Got anything? We haven't even talked to the press yet and you already know it's a double homicide." Barnes laughed sarcastically.

"It's a small town, I know it's different than what you're used to," the councilman excused.

"No matter, it's not like any details got out." Barnes relaxed. "No harm done. We've only got preliminary info at this point."

"I heard one guy got cut up pretty bad, stabbed in the back, and another guy was found with a broken nose and a knife in his eye? It sounds pretty gruesome," the councilman hinted.

"You heard that, huh? There was no knife in the eye, it was a broken nose. What kind of town have you got here, Jim?" Barnes challenged more than asked. "What have you gotten me into?"

Barnes and Jim Meyer had roomed together at Cal Davis and their friendship transcended the norm. In fact, it was almost unshakeable. Each felt as if they owed the other some kind of debt, though neither seemed to know why. Maybe it was the bond forged over the four years in the same dorm room, or perhaps it was the dirt they had on each other from their younger, wilder years. No matter, they were as close as brothers and trusted each other implicitly. The detective always found it odd though, that his tall, lean buddy could harbor such a deep and resonant voice. Didn't seem to match the outer dressing.

"What kind of town is it? What have I gotten you into, eh?" The councilman looked back and locked eyes with his detective cohort. "Well, at this point, I suppose it's the kind of town that needs answers, Brad. Answers from someone who has the experience and the savvy to take on a mess like this. What exactly is it you'd like me to say?"

"I don't know, Jim. Maybe you could tell me I'm dreaming and that I'm gonna wake up and finally get to that fishing you promised me when you drew me to come here in the first place?" Barnes didn't even like to fish...he didn't like the smell. The whole darn town smelled like fish, like fish and ocean. And paint.

"I'm sorry, Bud, you gotta know I didn't anticipate this" Jim sipped on his mug. "When Grimes checked out, we only had the kid. As smart and dedicated as he is, he just wasn't ready.

We thought we had more time…figured a couple of years with Grimes and he could take over when needed."

"Funny how things work out sometimes, you know?" Barnes said, spinning his mug again, exhibiting signs of frustration. "It smells like fish in here, Jim. And paint. Why does it smell like paint?"

"It's the moisture. We're down at the ocean. It's foggy and misty and wet. You gotta do a lot of painting to keep things looking nice," the councilman offered.

"Well, it's not a great combination, you know—fish and paint I mean." Barnes turned his nose up at his friend.

"You alright, Barnsie?" Jim lifted his mug and took another cold swig, looking slowly around the bar.

Barnes scratched at the base of his neck. "Yeah, I just…I kinda thought I left a lot of this behind me back in L.A."

The councilman put a heavy hand on his friend's shoulder, getting Barnes' attention. "You know, you didn't have to accept the position, Brad. You could've said no."

The detective stopped spinning his drink and turned directly to the councilman. "In what world do you live in that I could say no to you, Jimmy? You're the last good friend I have left," Barnes lamented. "Been married to the job so long…and with Patricia gone, I…"

"You know I'm grieving with you," his friend responded. "I didn't intend for the conversation to go in this direction. I'm just glad you're here."

He relaxed his shoulders and resumed spinning his drink. A couple of quarters clinked behind him as they were dropped into an old jukebox. There were some clicks and whirring as the machine searched out the request.

"She sent me here, Jim. We both know that. She knew I needed to be with friends," the detective whispered. "You're right I could've said no to the job. Dang Mayor didn't want me here, that's for sure. What was it he said? 'We don't need any hotshot, big city lawman in Rocky Point.'" He shook his head. "But the truth is, I didn't want to say no. For a whole slew of reasons, my loyalty to our friendship included." Barnes slogged down the rest of his second drink and waved the third on with the bartender.

"Maybe you should pump the brakes a little, partner," the councilman suggested. "And leave Mayor Moyer to me. He was just afraid that having a cop from L.A. up here would bring unwanted attention, that's all. I think he's warmed to the idea. You can still bug out if you want to, Brad? You've been through a lot, no pressure."

Barnes picked up a slice of lime from the dish at the end of the counter and twirled it carelessly in his hand. "No, this is what I do. I find clues and piece together puzzles."

Bartender Matt set the next mug of cold brew down and gave it a little push toward the detective.

Barnes moved the lime over the foamy head of his beer and squeezed. "I've been doing it so long, I don't know how to do anything else. I've gotta find the reasons. I have to squish the bad guys." He squeezed the lime wedge for effect.

Jim apologized. "Still, it was selfish for me to call on you. You came here to rest. But you're the only guy I trusted that could take us forward. The only guy I could count on to help mentor Colton and secure the department. It wasn't fair to you, I know that. And I'll never be able to thank you enough. Especially in light of what has happened out here today. But now, more than ever, the town needs your skill, knowledge, and expertise. Like you said, funny how things work out."

"It's okay, Jimmy." Barnes shifted in his seat. "I'm doing what I'm supposed to be doing. I'm okay with that. But I gotta tell you, I may be starting to crack."

"What are you talking about, You're the sanest guy I know." The councilman nodded.

"This afternoon at the beach, there was a picture of a girl. I can't get it out of my mind. I thought maybe it was just familiar because I'd seen a picture of her before in a case file."

The councilman looked puzzled. "And this is enough to rock your sanity? Seeing a girl that looks familiar?"

"Well, it is if she's dead," Barnes said, looking directly at his friend. "It was a picture of Doc Nichols' young wife."

The councilman appeared stunned. "Oh, Corrina. Yes, that was sad. Wait…are you telling me that the doc is involved in this thing out there today?"

"I think he's just a victim of very unfortunate circumstances at this point, but yeah, he was there," Barnes answered. "Maybe it's just the rush of being back on the job, I don't know, but that photo got me off balance."

"I'm sure that's all it is, bud. Just a little Deja Vu or something, the girl's been dead for months. It'll pass. Was there anything else odd out there?" Jimmie asked.

"The whole scene was odd, Jim. I've got a lot of thinking to do and a lot of questions to ask before I'm ready to form any real conclusions," Barnes answered.

"Well, if I can help in any way, you know where to find me, right?"

"There is something that you can do. I have names and some precursory information but I'm sure that you can give me a little more perspective."

"Feel free to stop by the office anytime. I'll be in all day. I'm not sure what you're looking for, but you know you can count on me." The councilman took a last sip and then patted his ol' roommate on the back. "But for now, I've got to say hi to a few folks, you know, duty calls."

"I never have figured out what it is that you like about politics, Jim," Barnes said, giving a casual wave as the councilman backed away from the bar.

"Someone's gotta do it. At least the bodies that I'm shaking are still breathing."

The hair on Barnes' neck stood up.

He finished the third drink and then another and one after that. When he finally left, it was late. He stepped outside the backdoor into the alley and turned his collar up against the slicing wind. He spotted his car and thought he saw movement. *A tall man in a dark suit?*

He squinted again into the dark night and decided he was seeing things.

CHAPTER 9

Prodded by a strange feeling, his head swooned in the fog of a dull throbbing as he ebbed into awareness. An icy, sharp sting inched its way quickly across his back and he just couldn't make sense of it. He lay motionless in the bed waiting for the sensation to pass. But like a million small needles, it pricked its way up his body. He tried to shake the cobwebs loose but as hard as he fought, he could not regain consciousness. He couldn't even move.

It was almost over his ears now, and from somewhere deep inside of him, a vice-gripping panic set in. *Water…freezing water, but how?*

He felt paralyzed but was keenly aware of his elevating pulse. His fight or flight mechanisms were racing, his adrenaline output in overdrive.

What the heck is happening? he screamed inside.

He could hear his erratic heartbeat in his ears now as the enveloping water continued to surge higher. Finally, his heavy eyelids sprang wide open. His eyes darted frantically around in their sockets, searching the small confines in terror. Under the glow of a single hanging light bulb, the paint-chipped, cold steel walls washed the room in a soft greenish-white, removing all detail. Not able to move, he scanned his body but couldn't see any restraints.

What the heck is going on? Am I on a ship? Are we sinking? He shook violently in protest as the water raised high enough to tickle his nose. Horror had taken on a whole new meaning.

This can't be happening. His mind raced, trying to remember how he'd gotten here. He acknowledged overdoing it at the bar after the investigation on the beach but couldn't recall anything since stepping into the cold night when he closed the place down. He remembered the man in black standing at the caution tape watching the investigation with intent and then perhaps getting to his car.

Who was he? Could he be involved? Barnes wondered.

He snorted in half a nose full of water and coughed. That sparked a guttural scream that started silently in his chest, exploding from his mouth as he regained some motor control and lifted his head slightly off of the bed. Water drained out of his ears and he heard a loud, hollow metal clanking sound outside the walls followed by a loud rumble. Like the roar of thunder, it rocked his senses.

He'd bought some more time, but only a little. The water was once again at the bottom of his nose and his sore neck strained to stay above it. His toes started to move and then his ankles. He was wiggling his feet in desperation. He tried to push himself off the table, but the rest of his body was not answering the call.

The water swept up over his nostrils just as he took one last tremendous breath. He was hoping to hold on long enough for the paralysis to subside so that he could get up and out of that cold place. Within seconds, it had overtaken his eyes and the freezing liquid stabbed at them like ice picks. He suddenly realized he was not going to get out of this, and he calmly relaxed his neck, allowing his head to float—listless.

As the blackness slowly engulfed him, through narrowing vision, he heard a loud beep. A second later, there was another loud beep and his body shook. A third echoing beep filled his cranium and he sprang up in his bed, gasping for air.

Outside the bedroom window of the granny flat he was renting, the trash truck's reverse alarm sounded. The huge vehicle shook the large bin on its forks before lifting it high and dumping the contents into the bay.

"Thunder," he cursed.

Sweat poured off of his forehead like a waterfall. He shook violently and pounded at the mattress in anger. His deep, rapid breathing began to slow as he realized it was just another nightmare—a dream inside a dream. How he hated those dreaded things.

Like the others he'd had…the one where he'd been skydiving only to realize his chute wouldn't open, or the one where he lay in a coffin and listened as his friends and family muttered goodbyes while shoveling dirt on top of him, he hated not being in control.

The therapist the department 'recommended' had said that, oftentimes, guilt over a loss could wreak havoc on a person's psyche. There could be panic attacks, depression, nightmares, or even delusions or hallucinations for some time after a traumatic event. Watching his wife slip away from him as he held her following that accident was the traumatic event.

It was my fault, I was driving. Why wasn't it me instead of her? It should have been me.

He shook away the guilt, thick as southern molasses, and his gaze quickly found the clock on the cable box. "Oh no! I'm going to be late."

Bounding from the bed to the bathroom in a single motion, he opted to rinse quickly in the shower and put off shaving in the interest of time. He was dressed and on the road to headquarters in less than 20 minutes.

CHAPTER 10

Barnes was lucky the roads were nearly empty. His tires held the wet pavement, slick with the remnants of the morning's moisture. The light turned yellow and he sped past a streetcar, noticing a difference in his reaction time when swerving to avoid a plastic trash can that blew across the road in front of him.

He swung the unmarked Crown Victoria into a slot near the front entrance, flattening some weeds that pushed through the black top, and hurriedly exited the vehicle.

His head felt heavy. If he tilted it too much to one side, it felt like it would pull him over. Every noise was amplified and ricocheted off of the wall of his cranial cavity. Even in the drizzle-grey of the clouded morning, his 250-dollar Rayban drivers were not effective enough to filter out the light and he had to squint to minimize the pain.

A glance behind him confirmed the storm front the radio announcer promised was quickly headed toward the coast. And much like the other morning at the beach, a cold morning offshore wind was at its head. But unlike the previous day, this gale had a temper, whipping at the town as if it was punishment.

The freezing air did little to quell the pounding in his head as he navigated the handful of steps to the department's entrance. He cursed when the wind grabbed the door from his hand, and it shut behind him with a loud slam.

He paused momentarily until the throbbing subsided. The scratchy shuffling of papers and the building chatter of voices waiting to get to the counter and be heard all stopped as they watched him hit the buzzer and walk through the small lobby into the station.

His sunglasses remained on, even though he was inside now—a dead giveaway to his hungover condition. He chose the shortest route to the detective area, careful to avoid being caught in any needless morning chatter. Patience was at a premium and he just wanted some personal space and a gallon or two of coffee to help him settle in. He thought about ducking into an interrogation room to rest for a few minutes in the dark and quiet but knew that was a bad idea as he might not want to come back out.

Down one hallway and through another corridor, he passed the print room. Until now, he'd never noticed the loud sound those stupid machines made as they echoed off of the hallways.

Despite his condition, he'd made it to work on time—something that was of paramount importance to him. It was a staple of his commitment.

But he was no match for his younger sidekick on this day. Having arrived an hour and a half ahead of his scheduled start time, Noble was already busy constructing an evidence board.

"Morning, Bradford," he yelled across the room without even looking up. He called him by his full name from time to time as a dig, just to get under his skin a little bit.

Barnes just raised a hand and fanned it, signaling both his greeting and discomfort. "Not today, kid. I don't have the patience."

Caught off guard, he looked toward his partner. "Uh oh, must've had a long night, huh?" Noble rose from his desk and turned to tack an index card to the chart.

"Yeah, I might have had one too many," Barnes whispered in response.

"You need some time or…?" Noble looked over his shoulder.

"Just let me grab some coffee and you can fill me in on what you have going there." Barnes eyed the board with indifference. "I've seen 'em on the TV. But we never had the space for something like that in L.A., too many cases going on at one time."

"Well, this is the only big one that we have right now, so I figured we could utilize the extra room," Noble responded.

At the coffee machine, Barnes grabbed a Styrofoam cup and started to fill it. Fingers found their way under his sunglasses, and he gently rubbed at his eyes. It felt so good that he forgot what he was doing for a moment. He raced to flip the plastic dispenser handle down but it was too late, he'd already spilled it over the top, burning his index finger.

"Crap, I should've stayed home today," he muttered under his breath.

"You okay, Brad?" Noble was reading the rap sheet on one of the two victims of the beach homicide.

"Yeah, yeah, just a little rough out of the gate today, kid." Barnes kept his composure—not to remain professional, but because he knew that any yelling would simply evoke more crushing pain behind his eyes. "Gimme a few minutes, huh?"

Noble took the fistful of papers and kept scanning over them. "No rush here, just doing a little light reading. Take all the time you need."

The savory scent of the warm blend filled his senses. He raised the cup of the thick, black brew to his lips and sipped at the potion that he hoped would aid in rejuvenating his energy. He took a few extra moments to get his game face on and allow him to catch up with the day. Satisfied that he was headed in the right direction, he grabbed another toothpick and sauntered to the evidence board. "Alright, kid, what do we have?

Noble had printed a few of the pictures from his tablet and pinned them up on the corkboard. Pictures of the doc's Mercedes and the paper evidence tents sat right in the middle, flanked by the light pole photos where they found the first victim, and the bluff where the second victim ended up. "Okay, we got the two dead guys, here and here," Noble pointed to the photos at opposite ends of the board. "And we've got the doc in the middle telling his story where he's at the beach reminiscing. But that's it…no other witnesses, at least not yet."

"Evidence?"

"Tests being run on the blood on the hood. We have beer cans on site, checking for DNA. The matchbox, a knife that's being printed, the blood on the car's armrest console, and the rest is thin," Noble answered. "Coroner is running toxicology as requested."

"What about those phones, did we find anything?"

"No phones to be found." Noble sat back down.

"Great. What else have we learned about the two victims since yesterday, what was it, Walker and Sutherland?" Barnes stirred his java and blew on it, trying to cool it down a bit while keeping his index finger extended, away from the heat.

"Yeah, IDs are confirmed. Mason Wells Walker is the dead guy in the parking lot. He's a therapist; only been in the Point a little over two years." Noble flipped a page over. "Works out of an office over on Canyon, a few blocks away. He looks really clean, legit. He's got a pretty impressive resume too, went to Pepperdine as a psych major, graduated Magna or some kind of laude. No wants, no warrants, and absolutely nothing criminal in his background. Not even a traffic stop."

"Squeaky clean, huh?" Barnes rocked on his heels.

Noble tapped the rap sheet. "Like someone 'whitewashed' him with bleach."

"What's he doing in Rocky Point, I wonder?" Barnes rubbed his chin. "Guy with those credentials could make a heck of a lot more money in a big city I'd think."

Out of the big bay window in the detective's office, lightning flashed in the clouds over the ocean, drawing Noble's attention. "No wife, no kids. You'd think he'd be looking for a better situation than this, I agree."

"Next of kin?" Barnes quizzed, moving toward the window.

"Contacted Walker's family last night. They'll be in town later today, took the first flight out." Noble flipped back to the front page. "I called them myself. Very proper sounding. Ivy league types from somewhere back east, you know, real upper crust. They were demanding answers before I'd even given them any details. I mean, it just happened, you know? Was strange," he added. "Not much in the way of emotion or anything…just wanted answers."

"Everybody reacts differently to this kind of news." Barnes tossed the coffee-dipped stirring stick into the nearest trash bin.

"My guess is that they'll be all over us until we can provide them a closed case," Colt tagged on.

Barnes had felt that strain before and it never improved the situation, only complicated efforts. "We'll have to meet with them as soon as they get in and ask for their patience and support up front. Maybe it'll provide us a little elbow room?"

"A good approach, Brad," Noble answered, enjoying the light show on the clouds.

"Yeah? Maybe, maybe not, but we don't need extra stress." Barnes turned back to the board Noble had constructed. "Have we learned anything else about dead guy number two?"

"Well, the matchbox you came up with kind of told the story on that one. He was a part-time bouncer at Lovergirls." Noble handed the rap sheet over to Barnes. "But this guy was a little harder to track. We can only find info going back a handful of years. Haven't even determined if he's got any aliases or 'other knowns' yet. We can't locate any next of kin or anything. Still waiting on the print searches."

"Lovergirls bouncer, huh? Didn't the doc say that he remembered this Walker guy stating the fight was over a girl?

Maybe these two were seeing the same woman? A dancer at the club would certainly make sense." Barnes flipped to the next page. "Wow."

"Yeah, I thought you might enjoy that." Noble anticipated the response.

"Assault, battery, burglary, a DUI, and a weapons charge. It's probably safe to assume that this guy was the aggressor." Barnes handed the sheet back.

"I've been kind of feeling all along that this was a simple murder attempt. A jealous boyfriend gone bad situation. Papers kinda point in that direction too, it would seem," Noble hinted.

"Well, let's keep digging. I asked the coroner to jump on this, just to be sure we're not missing anything." Flashing light outside the office window caught the older detective's attention. "I don't suppose we've heard anything on that yet?"

"Nothing yet, but I'm going with two deaths by stabbing. Come on, Brad." Noble laughed.

A few large raindrops began to pelt the window and dot the asphalt outside the station house. *It's getting real dark out there,* Barnes observed. "Yeah, Colt, it seems pretty straightforward I have to agree. We've got the doc down there to give us the play-by-play and wrap it all up nice and tight, right?"

"Look, I know we've got a couple of loose ends here, but this feels like a slam dunk to me. The background info points to it…the profile fits. Is it just me?" Noble asked.

"You're kidding, right, kid? It doesn't seem all too simple to you?" Barnes remarked.

"I'm confused. Am I missing something? Are you saying that the doc did it? Or someone else?" Noble sat down on the corner of a desk by the chart.

"No, kid, I'm not saying that the doc did or didn't do it. I'm saying we've got a lot of work to do to get a full picture of what happened here." Barnes became stern. "As an example, why the beach? If you're going to knock someone off, you usually pick a secure, private location. You know, no cameras, no outside influences, no danger of getting caught."

"You're overthinking this. It's not L.A.," Noble argued. "The background info is steering us to the logical conclusion."

Barnes pointed to the sheets. "If we only listened to the paper, we're not giving the case its due. You think this family that's flying out here is going to accept our speculation without some kind of facts to back it up? Besides, we've got this big case board you've set up and I'd hate to see all of the effort go to waste."

"Okay, that's real funny. But I'm going to go on record saying this one is simple. The bouncer did it because the rich therapist was banging his girl," Noble stated. "I hope we're not just wasting a lot of time and money. Please tell me you're not doing this for my benefit to teach me or something?"

"No, I'm not doing this to teach you anything. You're a fine detective with good instincts. And you may even be right, Colt, but we've got a process and procedures. We have an obligation to all parties and to the department, you know that," Barnes said respectfully.

"Of course, you're right. It just seems so clear with the information we have." Noble held up the rap sheets in his hand.

Barnes took a sip of his coffee and paused for effect. "Most often, it's the information that we don't have that is the most telling."

"I'm on record here though, right?" Noble verified.

"Yes, Colt, you are on record. And I sincerely hope you're right. Because if you are, this will all be finished very quickly," Barnes reinforced.

"Alright, what's next then?" Noble turned back towards his board. "We've got no witnesses except the old doc. He's certainly too old to have been able to take these two guys out. The cameras in the parking lot were a dead end. It's gonna be tough to get much more than we have in physical evidence."

"Cameras were a no-go, huh?" Barnes confirmed. "Shoot, I was hoping we'd get some tape on that…would've cut this thing to the quick."

"It seems they never worked, just for show." Noble shrugged.

"Well, we're going to have to do the leg work then, Colt. Let's go find out who these guys really are." Barnes shook his head at the evidence board. "Lovergirls probably won't open until later. So, we'll look at the therapist first and then get out to the dance club and see what we can find out about this Percival Sutherland character."

"Sounds good, Brad. I've got that dog poisoning thing over that way. You want to ride out with me or meet me there?"

Barnes took the last sip of coffee and tossed the cup at the trash bin, missing wildly. "I think I'll try and choke down a quick bite and see if I feel any better. Maybe try and pre-call the therapist's office to see if anyone's there. How about we plan to meet over there at about noon? I'll call if anything changes."

Noble let out a huge sigh. "Okay, I'll text you the address. Oh, wait…never mind, here, let me put it on a sticky note for you. You'll never make it by noon if you have to figure out how to read a text."

"Oh, so now you're the funny man? Noon kid, I'll see you there." Barnes' sarcasm was as thick as peanut butter. "Make sure you grab a heavy coat, it's looking nasty out there."

CHAPTER 11

The jostling wrested her from her fuzzy slumber. Or maybe it was the cold or the noise. They were moving now. She could feel bumps as the tires crossed over the dots when they changed lanes. The gentle rhythm of the vehicle as it glided over the pavement was like a lullaby, the dots were the percussion.

The warmth of her soft fuzziness had been invaded by the cold of the vehicle's interior where she lay. There were others, she could feel them next to her. She could hear their breathing and smell their body odor.

How long has it been? she wondered. She felt sticky like dried sweat had sealed her skin. She listened for the voices. Would the music of the vehicle have melody? No, there were none, there was no singing…there were no pretty words to keep her company.

She faded in and out as the road conditions dictated, or when one of the others rolled near during a turn and provided some warmth. Then she could return to her fuzzy rest. It was peaceful there, quiet…soft.

A loud thud. The vehicle must've hit some debris. Maybe one of those thrown tire treads or something and the subsequent swerving had shaken her awake. She tried to sit up but realized her hands were tied.

Someone in the vehicle must have heard her or seen her moving. Maybe they were checking after the loud interruption.

"Hey!" he yelled in a frantic wail. "One of them is moving."

He wasn't too far away, she could tell. His voice filled the space she was in. It was guttural, scratchy, and alarming. She wondered if he would hurt her, so she tried to twist away.

"Don't yell, you idiot!" came a voice from what she assumed was the driver's side of the vehicle. "You'll wake the others. Just give her this."

Give me what? What are they giving me? she squirmed. She heard a shuffling, a movement...*boots against steel.*

He was moving toward her slowly, avoiding stepping on the others. She could hear him getting closer, hear his laboring, the agitation in his breathing. She was already recoiling in fear when she felt the sting, the biting pain as the needle found her shoulder.

It was like ice was creeping through her veins and then it instantly turned to warmth.

Warm, soft, and fuzzy. She relaxed as a wave of peace crept over her and fell into unconsciousness again. A warm, soft, fuzzy slumber.

CHAPTER 12

In a steady but light rain, Barnes carefully took a green light and turned east off of Coast Highway onto Canyon Point Drive. Slowly rolling past the small shops that lined the two-lane drag, he acknowledged how beautifully maintained the most traveled area of town was. Large trees sparsely decorated the sidewalks, all neatly trimmed.

The shops were all in pristine condition with fresh paint on the outside and the windows clean under new colorful awnings. It was obviously a town continually on display. Everything from pottery stores and gift shops through surfboard and ocean wear to small restaurants filled the eclectic gauntlet from the coastal highway about half a mile or more inland. This was the pulse of the town, the place where most of the commerce that kept 'the Point' alive was done.

Almost all of the shops shared residence above the commercial space. He glanced at the dashboard and checked the time. He had arrived at 1221 on Canyon Drive at approximately 11:45 am. He found a diagonal parking space four or five spots shy of the therapist's office and pulled his black Crown Victoria within inches of the parking meter.

The rain had begun to intensify, so he took advantage of the extra time to read through the background information on Dr. Walker one more time before heading in.

Mason Wells Walker, he read. *Born April 17, 1987, in Connecticut, family still lived there. His record is unblemished. Got his degree in psychology at Pepperdine and then returned home to start a business.* He removed a printed digital photo from under a paper clip that his mom had emailed Noble after having informed them of her son's passing.

Good looking kid, Barnes thought. *Could've made it as an actor or something with those looks. He appears confident and friendly.* He was startled by a sudden knock on his window.

Outside, Noble leaned over with both hands in the pockets of his trench coat and squinted in the rain. "You ready? It's wet out here."

Barnes motioned him in. He unlocked the door as Noble darted across the front of the car and slid into the passenger seat next to him. "Everything okay, Brad?"

"Yeah, kid. I was just going over the paperwork on this guy," Barnes said, ruffling the sheets.

"You find something you don't like?" Noble felt a little pinch at his side. He shifted in the seat and removed his badge, setting it on the dashboard.

"Not necessarily, no. I'm just trying to get a better feel for who we're investigating. I mean, look at him." Barnes passed the picture over to his partner. "Almost looks like a model or movie star or something. I can certainly understand how this could've been a problem over a girl. He must've had to swat them away with a stick."

"Well, he doesn't have that problem anymore, that's for sure. I remember thinking the same thing after the photo came through. But what does that mean?" Noble asked.

Barnes scratched at the small whisker growth that he hadn't addressed that morning because of his hangover. "Well, it might not mean anything at all except that he was a good-looking guy. But it does occur to me that he could pick just about any girl and make out okay. So, why go after another guy's woman?"

"I don't know, Brad, maybe that's his thing?" Noble suggested. "Maybe he didn't know the girl was with someone else? Or maybe the bouncer went after his girl? Women have been known to play the field too, you know."

"Okay, I suppose you're right about that," Barnes agreed. "But I'm still a bit confused over the move to California. I know he went to school here…I get that. But his mom told you he had a business all set up in Connecticut. I wonder what made him bug out."

"We didn't get that far into the conversation. But judging from the parents' lukewarm reaction to the news of his demise, I'd say there wasn't a whole lot of love there. Maybe he just wanted to get away from them, you know, do his own thing his own way?" Noble offered.

"Once again, a good theory. Could be a lot of things, sure. But it's tough to build a business and get clientele. To close down a successful practice and move doesn't make a lot of sense." Barnes was tapping the papers against the steering wheel. "And what was it you said about this guy being squeaky clean? I mean, come on…32 years old and not so much a traffic violation?"

"Yeah, I see your point there. But maybe the business wasn't successful? I can go after some financials once we get the name of the company from his family. We can certainly dig a little deeper." Noble shifted anxiously in the seat.

"Already on it, called back there and got the county recorder to give me everything they had on this guy's practice. He said he knew exactly who the guy was the second I mentioned him." Barnes chirped. "That was interesting in itself."

"How long until we get that info?" asked Noble.

"Could be at the station now, could come in tomorrow, it's in the great State of Connecticut's hands at this point." Barnes fired up the engine and switched the defroster on to rid the windows of fogging.

"Well, I guess we can get into that when we get back there," Noble seemed eager. "So, how do you want to play this with the receptionist?"

"We talked a bit before I left the office, she seemed eager to help. She was absolutely horrified by the whole thing. I didn't even have to tell her...she was already aware. Seems she knows someone in the coroner's office." Barnes became frustrated. "You know, it's very hard to work a case that everybody has information on quicker, or at the least as soon as we do. Don't these people have lives?"

"It's not L.A., Brad, these folks—most of them anyway—have lived here a long time. There's a bit of a network. They're a tight-knit bunch." Noble had already opened his door a couple of inches to let some fresh air in. "But they're good people, Brad. They're real good people."

"Yeah? Tell that to Walker's parents. I'm sure they'll be impressed." His sarcasm dropped like a sledgehammer.

Noble looked out the window of the vehicle just as a woman raced past them, splashing her way to her car, trying to avoid the heavy raindrops. "We're just talking about a couple of guys here, Brad. It's not the representative condition of Rocky Point. This is the first homicide case we've had here in some time."

"Ah, crap." Barnes tapped his partner's leg with the folder. "You're right, Colt. Where I come from, there's a lot of bad. It's tough to let that go."

"It's alright, Brad. I understand," he said, looking at his phone. "It's noon straight up. We should probably get in there and talk to the receptionist."

"Assistant, Colt. She's the assistant," Barnes corrected. "I made the mistake of calling her a receptionist earlier and she set that record straight. She's an assistant. We need to get that right as we don't want to lose her cooperation."

"10-4, Barnsie, I'm clear on the title," Noble calmed. "So, good cop, bad cop, or good cop, good cop?"

"We're not 'playing it' at all. She came off as being pretty invested in the guy. That was easy to pick up on. It sounds like they were close. I'm guessing she had a thing for him or maybe they were intimate," Barnes surmised. "We're going to want to tread lightly and give her as much room as she needs."

He grunted as he opened his door and stepped out onto the street. He took a compact umbrella from the side pocket on the door just as a small trickle of cold droplets fell from a branch above and caught him flush on the crown of his head. "Ah, screw it." He almost threw the umbrella back into the vehicle. "She's expecting us. Let's get a move on."

CHAPTER 13

Barnes pushed a couple of three-quarters into the parking meter as they went by and Colton moved astride him. Before they could even get to the therapist's office, the door swung inward and a petite, young woman in her late twenties dressed in pajamas and a robe stepped to the side, inviting them in. He wondered how much more attractive she might be, save for the obvious signs of grief that her puffy red eyes and smeared makeup indicated.

"Right on time, that's nice," she quipped, cradling a cup of espresso. "Everything just goes so much more smoothly when people stay on schedule, right?"

"I suppose so." Detective Barnes offered a card. "I'm Bradford Barnes. I believe we spoke earlier, Miss Crawford?"

"You can call me Kayleigh, Detective." She set the card and her hot drink on the small table just inside the door. "Here, let me take your coats," she offered, extending her arms. "Come on, gentlemen, I'd like to keep the warm air in. It's awfully nasty out there."

Colton pushed by his partner. With his back to Miss Crawford, he rolled his eyes as she removed his coat. *Guess we know who ran the show here,* he thought.

Barnes was already looking deeper into the room, trying to gain any insights into the doc's personality. It was all very benign—a comfortable open space with hardwood floors and decorative rugs strewn about where the furniture sat. The wall hangings were ocean related with ships and beaches pictured. There were a few plaster castings of sailors or pirates hung about and a very beautiful ship model of exquisite detail on display just outside the room marked with 'Office' over the door. He wondered how anybody could find the time or the patience to craft such an object.

"Alright, it's your turn, Mr. Barnes. Come now, relinquish your coat, I don't want to pay to heat the whole town," Kayleigh pretty much ordered.

After Barnes stepped in, she closed the door behind him and hung the wet coats on wooden pegs, kicking a small rug underneath to catch any drippings. She retrieved her coffee mug and a nearby tissue box, then led the detectives into the waiting area of the office.

The detectives sat down on an antique tan couch that had animal claws clutching a round-shaped wooden ball for legs before she rested on crossed legs in a high-backed chair herself. She regarded the two officers over her mug as she slowly sipped at the warm brew.

"I know this must be hard for you, Miss Crawford. Kayleigh, I mean." Barnes took out his small pad and stubby pencil to a sigh from Noble. "It's never easy to cope with a loss like this, but it's especially difficult when it is sudden and under peculiar circumstances. I don't mean to impose, but from our brief conversation this morning, I got the impression that the two of you may have been close?"

"Well, I was closer to him than he was to me, I guess." She shifted uncomfortably in the chair. "When I took the job, there were no clients. He had just moved here. He hadn't even opened the place yet." She pulled a tissue from the box and dabbed at her leaking eyes. "He said he couldn't afford to pay me right away because he spent everything he had in escrow, here. But he talked about how he wanted to help people get free from the things that imprisoned them with a passion that was so compelling." She grabbed another tissue and sobbed, turning toward the office door as she wiped her chaffing nose. She stayed quiet for a while.

The detectives sat quietly and patiently. Noble finally broke the silence. "Miss Crawford, if there's a better time for you, we would have no problem postponing the visit." He felt a pat on the back from Barnes.

Seeming completely adrift, she closed her hand over her mouth and both officers could see the tears falling off of her face. Barnes looked at his partner, closed his pad, and tucked it into his coat pocket. The two of them were rising from the couch when she stopped them. "No, please don't go. I'm sorry. It's just so fresh still, you know? I've been here alone since Clark called me yesterday. You know, the guy from the coroner's office I told you about."

Barnes returned to the couch. "Take as much time as you need, Miss Crawford. There is no rush." Of all the parts of his job, this was the most challenging to him. Not that he was dispassionate, just unsure of the correct personal approach to help people who were grieving. *Crud, I haven't even learned how to cope with my own wife's death.*

"I feel like I'm falling apart. Weird things are happening, I haven't gotten any sleep, I just…I don't even know what to do."

"Perhaps talking might help a little," Barnes suggested. "How long have you worked with Dr. Walker? What was your role here?"

"Oh, about two years now, I suppose. I do just about everything except work with the patients. Scheduling, collections, billing, light bookkeeping, even some transcription at times." She glanced around the office. "I did whatever Mason needed me to. He was such a great guy. He let me move in here until I started collecting a paycheck to help me make ends meet. He said I was just what he needed—someone organized and thorough." She continued, "He was right, of course, organization was definitely not his strong suit." She forced a tiny smile. "I was hesitant at first, but I needed the job and was already so far behind on bills, without any prospects."

"Hesitant, Miss Crawford?" Barnes relaxed into the couch, sensing this could go on awhile.

"Yes, he was going to be living here and I hardly even met the man. I'd never roomed with anyone but girlfriends in the past." She paused and stared into her coffee mug, idly stirring it with an undersized spoon. "And worse, I was attracted to him. I knew I couldn't show it or I'd lose the job opportunity."

"But he must have sensed it?" Noble quizzed.

"Well, if he did, he never let on to me. He kept things professional," Miss Crawford recalled. "I'd run out of any savings and was going to lose my apartment, so the argument with myself was short. I really didn't have much choice, you see."

"So, you took the job and moved in?" Noble had taken his tablet out and was tapping lightly on the screen, logging notes."

"It was so very exciting. He had shared his vision with me and told me that, together, we were going to build a practice that this community would welcome and be proud of." Kayleigh looked at Barnes directly. "Something special that the town needed, you know?"

"And did you, Miss Crawford?" Barnes returned her gaze.

Kayleigh went back to stirring the coffee. "Oh, at first, it was slow. But after we got that initial handful of patients, things picked up rather quickly. Even he was surprised with how rapidly the clientele base grew. It's not a huge metropolis, right?"

Barnes knew that he would have to be careful as they moved on from there. He thought briefly before going down the rabbit hole and exploring any relationship questions. "So, he was eventually able to offer you a salary?"

"Oh, yes, and he was very generous indeed," she answered quickly. "Within a few months, I was collecting a regular check."

"But you continued to live here?" Barnes suggested, addressing her current choice of attire.

"This? Huh…oh yeah. Like I said, he told me I could stay here as long as I needed. Maybe save a bit of money and build a little safety net if I wanted."

"You never left then?" Noble jumped in.

As she talked, Barnes scanned the room, looking for anything out of the normal, and settled on the bookshelf over her shoulder. The title jumped out at him. MENTICIDE – A Mind Bending Study.

"Well, it wasn't long after when things began to change around here. Sometimes we'd sit around after a long day and drink some wine together, you know, to unwind a little," Kayleigh continued, not sure if honesty was the best policy here. Quite frankly, she was a little embarrassed by this confession. "On one of those occasions, things went a little bit further than I intended."

"You were intimate, the two of you?" Barnes assumed.

"Oh no—heck no." She grabbed another tissue from the box and the waterworks recommenced. "I thought we had something special, but try as I might, I couldn't seem to get him interested."

"But you never moved out? Was that not uncomfortable?" Barnes pressed.

"He was always very good at keeping the business separate from the other," Kayleigh sobbed out. "I thought maybe he was just struggling with the arrangement. So, I tried to give him space. But he never talked about it, and I couldn't get him to open up. Huh, imagine that…a therapist that wouldn't talk."

"Probably not all that uncommon," Noble observed. "I mean, after talking all day long."

"You want uncommon?" she responded. "How about a pathetic receptionist who threw herself at a guy who couldn't even see her?" she ranted. "I should've left. I should've left the job and the house. Oooh!" she screamed and cried together. "Instead, I'm walking around half-naked, hoping he'll take me."

The awkwardness filled the room. Barnes wasn't exactly sure how to respond, so he just pushed through.

"I'm sorry, Miss Crawford. I know this must be hard. We're almost finished here," Barnes consoled. "I just have a few more questions. Can you tell us if he ever had any trouble? You know, maybe a patient that was unstable or any other kind of threats or anything?"

"I think we're all a little unstable, Detective. You are paying attention, right?" Kayleigh laughed. "But no, he didn't have any enemies that I was aware of. He came here to help people and kept pretty much to the script. I actually felt a bit guilty in the end, like perhaps I'd derailed him a little. He seemed different after that."

Barnes redirected his questioning. "Of course, we'll want to look at the scheduling books at some point. You said he acted differently. Maybe the change was due to something else. We'll be looking for any new patients or even scheduling changes—anything that might help to figure out what happened at the beach yesterday."

"Well, I'm not sure what I can give you, patient confidentiality and all considered. But I can tell you that he's only had three new clients in the past quarter or so." Miss Crawford stood up, sensing the meeting was ending. "I feel a little torn, I don't want to do anything wrong. Mason was very protective of client information. I don't think it's right to just hand that over."

"Miss Crawford," Barnes said, pulling himself up off of the couch. "I think we've taken enough of your time for one day. If there is anything else you think might be helpful, please give us a call. The number is on the card."

"Of course, Detectives. Let me get your coats for you," she said, shuffling toward the door.

"Are you okay here? Is there anything we can help you with?" Noble inquired.

"Me? Oh…uh, I'll be okay A bit of an overactive imagination right now, but I'll be fine," she said, opening the door to a cold rush of air.

Barnes thought hard to resist asking, "An overactive imagination?"

"Oh, I'm sure it's nothing but I keep thinking I'm seeing the same people walk by here, looking in, standing around."

"Perhaps we should get a black and white to cruise by a few times a day? Might make you feel a little safer," Noble offered.

"No need for that. I'm sure it's nothing. Mason would've said it was just my mind coping with the emotional stress and a lack of sleep." Kayleigh thanked them and helped them on their way.

The detectives took their coats and moved under the awning after thanking the assistant again. "Where to next, Barnsie?" Colt quizzed, flipping his collar up against the weather.

"We're going to need to look at those books to see the patient list. We've also got the guy's family flying in today too, right?" Barnes stated, inserting a toothpick.

"Their flight gets in around 3:30. I told them to check in and then give us a call. We can meet with them at the station later, I suppose?"

"Let's meet on their turf, they'll be more comfortable," Barnes said. "I'm going to give Jimmy a call over at city hall. Maybe drop by for a visit and get a warrant ready if we need it." There was a pause. "You ever heard of menticide?"

"Nope, not a word I'm familiar with. Why?"

"Probably nothing. Let me make that call."

"All right, well, I finished the dog thing, so I'll head back and see if that paperwork came in from Connecticut. Meet you for a bite before we meet the Walkers?"

"Sounds good," Barnes threw his wet overcoat in the trunk. "Gimme a call around four or so." He turned his phone on and dialed the commissioner to let him know he might need a warrant or two. *The folks at Lovergirls might not be so helpful, and we're going to need access to the doc's records.*

CHAPTER 14

The unmarked medical transport vehicle turned into a commercial area and headed to the last building at the end of the business cul-de-sac. They'd chosen the building because it was the most secluded. Around the back, the vehicle rolled to a stop at the rear entrance of the offices under the purposely broken security light.

The gentle sound of water lapping at the rocks of a small jetty now replaced the sound of the van's loud engine. It washed away the smell of gas with the sting of salt water and told her they were near the ocean.

When the van's back doors swung open, the biting night air that whipped through the interior pulled at her consciousness, but she did not move.

The guy with the gruff voice spoke in a low tone, "I'll go get the cart. You wait here."

She heard the wheels wobbling as the gurney and the angry-sounding man neared the van. Then the scraping sound as they dragged the first of those in the vehicle toward the back doors and loaded them onto the transport.

Wobbling wheels again and then quiet. A match struck against a box and the faint aroma of marijuana wafted into the vehicle.

It all came back. The heavy scent of pot had triggered her... reached a part of her mind where important, deep memories were stored. She was flooded with emotion. The boy in her bed, the joints they shared, the laughing and playing, and the sweet sticky smell of sweat and sex. Then her mom bursting in and dragging her out, yelling at the boy to leave. But it was the argument in the aftermath of that drama that was pulling at her.

"You look at me when I'm talking to you!" her mom ranted.

"Mom, you're being ridiculous." She recalled the emotional afternoon, choking back tears that threatened to smear eyeliner over her softly freckled cheeks. "I'm 16. I'm not a child anymore. You can stop trying to control me now."

"As long as you live under my roof, you follow my rules, young lady." Her mom raised her voice another notch.

Here we go again, Reagan thought, rolling her eyes as the words echoed in her head. "I know, Mom. As soon as I get a job and start paying rent, I can make my own decisions," she mocked.

"Good, I don't even have to say it then. We understand each other." Her mom stood tall, straightening the company realty jacket on her dark blue Anne Klein pantsuit—an attempt to appear composed.

Then she recalled the times in the dark room, wondering about an argument...maybe her mom. But the smock had told her that her mom was gone, that they were all gone. She questioned again if she had hurt her mom, if this was what caused her schism.

"It was just a joint, Mom, that's all. It's not like I'm doing heroin or something." Her unkempt brown ponytail bounced as she became more animated.

"You can't possibly be serious?" Anger flushed her mom's entire face to a deep crimson. "You were supposed to be in school. Instead, I come home early from work to find you naked in your bedroom, smoking pot with a boy two years older than you."

"You didn't need to be so rude, Mom."

"Sure, Reagan, maybe I should have offered him a beer, or perhaps a condom or two. Do you think I'm an idiot? That I don't know what's going on with you?"

Reagan, my name is Reagan. Why were they calling me Rachel? What is going on? Her head was swooning, then back to that day with her mom.

"Do you think I'm an idiot, Mom?" She was not giving in, and the conversation continued to escalate. "Like I haven't seen you smoking pot and getting drunk with all of your 'friends' that you've been bringing home? At least I can still say I've never snorted coke."

She remembered her mom leaning forward onto the butcher's block, letting her head droop. She knew she was pushing the limits. Anticipation swelled as she watched long, dye-blond, curly locks sway as her mom wrestled with her thoughts.

Then it came. Reagan could sense that patience had worn through, and tolerance had no place left in her mother when she unleashed the full force of her fury in the face of what she felt was an unnecessary, vicious attack.

"You unappreciative little shit!" Reagan noticed her mom's head rise almost imperceptibly. She shook when eyes stoked with the rage of betrayal that only a loved one could ignite locked on her. "You have no idea what I've been through. I would appreciate a little respect. I've broken my back taking care of you and your sister since that piece of trash left us."

"He didn't leave us, Mom…he left you!" the 16-year-old lashed back. "You drove him away with your controlling ways and the drinking. And you haven't learned a thing."

The shaking was visible, more noticeable than ever before. She couldn't remember ever seeing her mom this mad. Since her older sister had left, her need for freedom and her mother's inability to let go had come to this. She now sought independence from a woman who had waited too long to attempt to instill discipline and was determined to draw the line here—now.

"So, you think you've got this all figured out, huh?" She watched her mom fold her arms and cock her head to the side. The anger in her tone reverberated off of the kitchen walls. "All of a sudden, you're a genius now? Oh, right, I forgot. You've smoked a couple of joints and screwed a boy. Hello, Einstein."

"Whatever." Reagan sensed things were spiraling out of control and dismissed the rant.

"I've worked two jobs so that you have a safe place to sleep and food to eat! I made something out of myself." The floodgates broke and water streamed from her eyes.

"Oh, okay, thanks for the food then," the sarcasm oozed.

"I didn't do it for thanks. I did it for you girls. Aargh!" Her mom spun around. "And you've taken it all for granted. You're cutting class and doing drugs? What's happened to you? You're ruining your life! Can't you see that?" She dabbed at her wet eyes with a folded paper towel.

"It was a harmless joint, Mom. I was just having a little fun." Reagan got up and adjusted her pink and white 'Hello Kitty' pajamas before retreating toward the safety of her room.

"STOP, Reagan! We're not done here!" her mom yelled after her.

"Maybe you should try some Xanax or something, Mom," Reagan quipped. "What are you getting so crazy about?"

"I'm crazy because of you. You're supposed to be my baby girl." Her breathing had turned to panting. As much as she tried to relax, calmness evaded her. "I can't stand idly by and watch you make stupid mistakes before you're even old enough to know what you're doing, sweetie."

"Oh, so now I'm stupid? Is that what you're saying?" She turned at the edge of the kitchen.

"No, I'm saying your choices are stupid. You're not seeing clearly right now," her mom argued. "Your grades are dropping, and you don't even seem to respect yourself. You don't want to end up being addicted to alcohol or drugs, and you certainly don't want to be a slut, do you?"

"It seems to have worked for you." It just came out. She wished she could grab that sentence back as soon as it had escaped from her mouth. She wanted to make a point, yes, but even she realized her mistake.

The words swept through the room like floodwaters. Reagan recognized it as a tidal wave of anger overcame her mom and she could only see red as the blood boiled inside. Her intentions were unmistakable as she charged her daughter.

Reagan was not backing down and raised her arms to defend against the onslaught. She let out a high-pitched scream as her mother easily broke through the defenses and grabbed two fistfuls of hair. She lifted her daughter off the ground and sent her careening over the sofa in the adjoining room.

When she finally managed to scramble back to her feet, there was no getting away. Her mom was right there, on top of her, puffing like a locomotive. Spittle flew from her mouth as she ranted, "You're just an ignorant, uncaring little shit!" They scuffled wildly across the living room, knocking the coffee table over and breaking a lamp.

"Mom, leave me alone! What's wrong with you?" They continued to struggle against each other until her mom tired and released her grip. Reagan thought it was over. Her mom stepped back and measured her daughter one more time.

The sting from the brutal slap across her face meant nothing compared to the pain she felt inside. It was as if she was melting away. She stood there for a few seconds looking through the sweat-soaked strands of hair her mom had tried to tear from her head.

Her mother instantly recoiled, her hands against her face. Horrified by what she had done, she tried to reach for her daughter, "Reagan, I'm so sorry…"

"I hate you!" She paused. "You're not my mom. You're just a pathetic old hag!" Reagan bolted from the living room."

"No, Reagan, please," she called after her. "Reagan, I'm sorry. I'm so sorry." The door to her room slammed shut and she collapsed to the floor, sobbing uncontrollably.

Just like that, the bond between mother and daughter had evaporated. She remembered being so angry that her mom could not gather herself together enough to protest when, minutes later, she raced through the hallway and burst out the front door in a thick hooded sweatshirt. She was still angry. But this time, she was angry with herself. She wished she could take it all back, go home and give her mom a hug. They could work it out, she was certain.

Instead, she remembered the hastily prepared backpack that hung on one shoulder. Her swollen face, the canvas for eyes wet and puffy, squinting against the waning sunlight until she plucked some sunglasses out of her pack and slipped them on. *Never coming back,* she told herself, and then dashed out of sight.

It came back as a blur, her navigating the residential streets of her neighborhood to get to the larger city thoroughfares. She remembered tapping frantically at her phone, texting the boy she had shared the joint and the bed with.

When he responded, she was standing on the corner of a downtown intersection.

The tears had started again, and she trembled gently as a light rain fell. He told her to meet him at the bus station and that they would go away together and figure things out. She felt a sudden sense of relief.

A moment later, a small sedan pulled up next to her and the window rolled down. "You look like you've had a tough day. Is there somewhere I can take you? Perhaps a cup of coffee? We can talk if you like?"

Sensors on alert, Reagan stepped back and looked at the driver. She calmed immediately when she saw his attire. The encounter became crystal clear in her memory.

"Well, I have to get to the bus station on the other side of town," she said, almost completely exhausted. "But I don't want to bother you."

"No bother, it just appeared that you were going to get awful wet in the rain," the man replied. "As you can see, I'm always ready to help."

"Are you sure?"

"I'm certain, but it's up to you?" he reassured.

"I guess it'll be okay. I mean, obviously it'll be okay," she responded.

"Well, you should get in before you get too wet," he urged as the car's door swung open.

She looked back toward home, took a deep breath, and slid into the passenger seat, placing her backpack on the floor. "I'm just going to send a text to let my sister know I'm leaving for a while." She leaned forward to get her phone.

When she sat up, the chloroformed handkerchief enveloped her face. He easily restrained her as she fought to stay conscious. 'Never going back, never going back...' the words reverberated in her head and she looked in horror into dark, vapid eyes before blacking out.

***

Now she knew she was in a desperate position. She'd been kidnapped, drugged, and hypnotized or re-programmed—brainwashed. She hated that she realized she had a role in the argument. Tears welled in her eyes. She needed her mom...she just wanted to go home.

Her fear spiked but she stayed calm. Her hands were zip-tied but her legs were free. When the cart returned, they dragged another body out of the van. On the way back into the building, the gurney tipped, cutting the corner in a rush. The gruff man cursed, "Crap. Gimme a hand, will ya? I can't get her back on this thing, we're pinned."

The driver of the van reluctantly went to help, and Reagan slipped out unnoticed. With no idea of where she was or where she was going, she ran as fast as she could into the black night. In the distance, she saw a light, a dim lamp, a beacon. She didn't even look back. Her bare feet ached with every step onto the rough gravel road, but she kept on running, trying to be as quiet as she could.

CHAPTER 15

"Commissioner Meyer, there's a Detective Barnes here to see you," buzzed the voice over the speaker.

The councilman finished tapping on his keyboard, "Oh, great, send him right in, Annie," he said, removing his reading glasses and tucking them into a nearby case. He was on his feet in a flash, moving around his desk to greet his friend with a firm handshake as he opened the door. "How are you doing, Brad? I was a little worried about you last night." He lightly patted his back.

"Thanks, Jim." Barnes nodded. "Yeah, I'm sorry about that. I've got a lot of stuff weighing on me right now. Throw a little lager into the mix and you never know what can happen."

"Well, here," Meyer said, leading him toward one of the leather chairs that sat opposite the dark walnut desk in his expansive city office. "Grab a seat and take a load off for a minute or two. How is your headspace, bud?"

"I'm fine." Barnes sank into the soft cushion and repositioned the new toothpick he had just inserted. He quickly scanned the room, reacquainting himself with the décor. It was a sparsely decorated workspace except for the overstuffed bookcases lining one entire wall and a custom credenza on the other side of the room. A couple of expensive-looking paintings hung on the wall on either side of the councilman's law degree, which had been framed and was matted in a dark green, chosen to accent the walnut cabinetry. "I hate to barge in on you this way, but I thought I'd try to pick your brain on these two victims from the beach?"

"Oh, sure. Of course." Jim moved back behind his desk and pulled out the reading glasses again. "Yeah, it's getting harder and harder to see each day." He shrugged.

"That's not the half of it, Jimmy." Brad scoffed without the need to go into further detail.

"Let's see, yes, I got an email right here from you earlier," he said, slipping the lens onto his long face. "Mason Walker and Percival Sutherland, right?"

"That's them."

"Well, I'm not sure what I can tell you about either of them, Brad. Only met one of them actually. Walker came here about a couple of years ago. He filed for a business license. I remember when it came across my desk that we didn't have much in the way of mental health support around here."

"I imagine if a guy plans on opening a surf shop, there's not too much to ask about," Barnes reasoned. "But what about a professional like this? Is there a background check or some qualification process before a guy sets up shop?"

"Oh yeah, and I remember he was pretty anxious to get rolling, too," Jimmy recalled. "He phoned or visited the hall here fairly regularly while he was waiting for the license. But if I remember correctly, he checked out as very clean."

Barnes was reaching for his pad. "Did you ever get to spend any time with him?"

"Only a couple of occasions that I can recall," Jim thought for a minute. "Once here, of course, and once at a silent auction for benefit somewhere in town. Sharp guy, very friendly, and I remember the ladies being pretty keen on him."

"How was he as far as the business was concerned…I mean, no complaints or trouble?" Barnes pressed.

"Not that I can think of," Jim answered. "But these days, something like that would probably come through YELP or a blog of some sort, so you can try looking there. Well, unless of course the police were involved, but then you'd have known that. I don't recall the guy being very social. Never saw him out at dinner or a club or even in the gym. Think he stayed pretty close to home base, kind of a workaholic type."

"Oh, yeah, he was working alright," Brad half spoke.

"What's that?" The councilman said cupping his ear.

"Uh, how about this other guy?" Brad flipped the page on his pad. "Percival Sutherland, you know of him?"

"I'm sure I'm familiar with a whole lotta people in this area but I'm afraid that's a name I just don't recall ever hearing. Is he from Rocky Point? Does he live here?" the councilman queried.

"He's a bouncer over at Lovergirls. It's a strip joint on the outskirts of town."

"I'm familiar with the place." He laughed. "I'm old, not dead."

"Well, that's too bad. I really hoped you might have at least something on either of them. In that case, like I told you, Colt and I will need to head out there later and see what we can dig up. Any news on that warrant?"

"Working on that, but it may take a little time."

Barnes set his notepad on the table next to him. "Jim, I really don't want to put you out but if you have anything on the background you ran on Walker, I'd love to get a look at it. Just want to be thorough, you know?"

"Sure, Brad, no trouble at all," Jim responded, sliding his seat to the desk's edge. He punched on the speaker phone and Annie chimed in immediately. "Hey, Annie, can you call over to records for me and ask for any information on a Mason Walker…he had a therapist office down on Canyon Drive I think?" he said, looking at Barnes for confirmation.

Barnes nodded.

"Of course, Mr. Meyer," she answered.

"Thanks, Annie, I'd appreciate any haste you could muster." The councilman clicked away and then decided to change course. "Brad, listen, I know this is hard. Patricia was so special."

"You know, she told me if anything ever happened to either of us, we should beat a hasty retreat to Rocky Point and look you up. We were going to retire in four years. We were actually thinking of settling somewhere like this, she often talked about you and Char. Who knows, we might've ended up here," Barnes rambled.

Jim's face showed concern. "You guys were together a lifetime. I can't even imagine. I know you can't just shut off the feelings, but keeping busy might help. You know I'm always available to talk if you need me."

"I appreciate that, Jim. I really do."

"Hey, you remember the time the four of us went out to Santa Barbara that weekend?"

"State Street, right?" Brad smiled for the first time since arriving.

"We tore that town up," Jim laughed.

"Woke up the next morning as I recall on a silver streak pulling into Seattle, Washington," Barnes chortled. "Not one of the four of us knew how the heck we got there."

"Didn't even slow us down though, did it? A little hair of the dog and some sunglasses and we kept that party alive." Jim was almost beaming. "Charlene was always so uptight until then. After that, she just kind of came out of her shell."

"You guys were great together, Jim." Barnes leaned forward.

"Still are, Brad. She loved Patty too. It's a shame we didn't find a way to get together more often." Jim tapped a pen on his wrist.

"I love you like a brother, Jim." Barnes scratched at his neck. "I wish we'd have made more of an effort too. Not like we were gonna get them to flash the conductor again when the train pulls out of the station." Barnes leaked a tear out of the corner of his eye.

The councilman rocked back in his chair and put his arms behind his head. "I wouldn't trade those times for any amount of money. Man, if you could just go back and relive a period of time?"

"Yeah, the Groundhog Day wish." Barnes nodded slowly. "Yeah, that would be a good time to get all 'Punxsutawney Phil.'"

Jim was just about to start down another memory lane when a knock came at the door. "Come in," he said in his big booming voice.

"I hope I'm not interrupting anything. It sounds like you guys are having a great time in here?" A very tall and curvy blonde woman slipped into the room. "I understand you are looking for some information?"

"Sara," blurted the councilman. "How fortuitous, you must know Detective Barnes, I'm sure?"

"I'm sorry, I haven't had the pleasure," Barnes said, reaching out to shake her hand but turning his head toward his friend in confusion."

"Well then, let me do the honors," offered the councilman. "Sara Noble, this is Brad Barnes, one of my oldest and closest friends."

"Well, I finally get to meet the legend," Sara said proudly. "Oh, Colton just cannot stop talking about you, Mr. Barnes."

Barnes was almost in awe of her overall presentation. The picture of professionalism, dressed in a nice dark blue pantsuit, she had a sort of regal look about her. Her posture was exquisite, and even with the librarian glasses on, there was no mistaking her natural beauty. "Ms. Noble, it's nice to finally meet you. Colton is your biggest fan."

"Aw, go on, Mr. Barnes. I mean, go on, please." She laughed like they were old pals.

"Brad, Sara here has been with City Hall for over 15 years." Jim clasped his hands together. "She's done everything from working in the courthouse to clerk and recorder. As a matter of fact, that's where she met Colton, and the rest, as they say, is history."

"Well, don't make it sound so simple, Mr. Meyer." She blushed. "It wasn't like a whirlwind romance or anything but there is a little more to it than that. It was a hot summer day, actually. I was at the courthouse, in a hurry to get back to the office here. I came out and found a flat tire on my car. Colton was there testifying on a case. When he was leaving, he must've heard me cursing like a rusty old sailor and that knight in shining armor came to my rescue. Just when I thought things were going to be okay, he let me know my spare tire was flat. So, he dropped me at the office, fixed the spare, changed the tire, and brought me back at the end of my shift. I was hooked."

"Wow, that is some story." Barnes unbuttoned his coat. "I knew there was something about that kid that I liked."

"Well, he likes just about everything about you, Detective. Says you're a regular genius on the streets. Maybe we should have you over for some supper sometime, Mr. Barnes?"

"That would be fantastic. I haven't had a real meal since I got up here," Barnes said. "On your schedule, of course."

"I'll look forward to that." She smiled. "Well, anyway, boys, I'll let you get back to your fun, but here is the paperwork you requested, Councilman." She handed the folder to the councilman and spun on her heels, winking as she turned. "I hope it helps. And by the way, I called in a favor. The warrant you requested for the search of the therapist's office is tucked in there also. You can pick up the one for Lovergirls in the morning. Judge is a friend of ours."

"Thanks so much, Ms. Noble. I'm off to rendezvous with your man then. We've got an appointment with the therapist's family. I hate these situations."

CHAPTER 16

Tall, thick pines lined the twisting, turning road up the hill. Slivers of sunlight cut through the branches and danced over the highway, reflecting off of the drizzling rain while the storm temporarily abated. Dusk settled in and the temperatures began to drop rapidly.

The Crown at Rocky Point was the poshest hotel in the area. The huge, luxurious facility was located in the southernmost part of town. The city council was bent on ensuring that the quaint and historic nature of Rocky Point remain completely undisturbed and would only approve new construction on the outside of the district.

Taking over two years to construct, it was painstakingly built among the beautiful coastal pines with an eco-friendly approach that strived to ensure any tree that was too small to use in the log cabin-style construction be removed and transplanted elsewhere in the nearby forest. Two environmental surveys were completed prior to commissioning the project and a slew of endangered species of wild toad had to be relocated as well. The result was one of the most beautiful and seamless integrations of modern technology and comfort ever imagined.

The detectives pulled under the huge, covered parking entrance at the front of the building. They marveled at the beautiful construction as real logs chinked together and covered in Linseed oil, set over three feet of stone, greeted them. It was both rustic and elegant at once.

Barnes handed the keys to one of the valets and offered him a crisp $5 bill. The gentleman half smirked, exchanging the numbered end of his ticket, which was quickly slipped into the breast pocket of his coat. *The hotel obviously attracts a high-end visitor,* Barnes made note.

Through the large automatic door, the two detectives made a beeline straight for the registration counter. "Would you please buzz the Walkers and let them know that we're here?"

"I would love to," the effeminate service representative behind the computer sarcastically responded. "But I'm afraid I don't know who 'we' are."

Noble pulled out his badge and said, "Just let them know that the detectives are here to see them, thanks."

"Oh, of course, no problem," he answered with a much more professional tone to his voice.

The detectives turned around and took in the richly decorated lobby. Ornate chandeliers hung from tremendous wooden beams aloft the real hardwood flooring. Beautiful hand-woven rugs sat under finely crafted furniture made from the timber cut on the site. Tremendous, framed mirrors hung on the walls, giving the appearance of even more vast, spaciousness. The lobby split into three separate wings, all of which had to be kept under three stories to avoid eclipsing the canopy of pines and destroying the view. No expense had been spared.

After a few minutes, an elevator dinged, and a gentleman dressed in all black wearing sunglasses exited and made his way toward the detectives. He checked the lobby in all directions as he sauntered across the room. Barnes noted the black suit immediately, wondering if he may have been the man at the beach.

"Gentlemen, I'm Agent Wright," he said in a monotone voice. "I'm assigned to the senator and Mrs. Walker. Come this way, please."

They tucked in behind the agent and headed back toward the elevators. Barnes looked sternly at Noble, who shrugged and mouthed, "I didn't know?"

The agent motioned and they all stepped into the elevator. Agent Wright moved to the back and stood with his arms together at his waist, legs apart with his eyes straight forward. He didn't appear as if he was interested in small talk.

"So, Senator Walker, huh?" Barnes broke the ice.

"That's correct, sir," the agent responded. "Second-term, second-generation. He's got quite the reputation…a no-nonsense guy."

"I'll remember that," Barnes thanked him.

"Thought it might help." He stared forward coldly.

The elevator reached the third floor and the agent reached out and pulled the emergency stop button. He took out a key and inserted it, turning it to the left.

Both of the detectives were surprised when it opened behind them. They stepped out into a very big hall where only three doors were visible.

"The senator has reserved the whole side of the floor," informed the agent, advancing out to his right. "He and Mrs. Walker are rooming at the other end." He pointed the other way down the hall. "We'll be meeting on the north side of the wing."

After getting the detectives situated in the living room of the nearest suite, Agent Wright moved behind the adjoining room's door, and just before disappearing, said, "The senator will be with you shortly."

Barnes waited about 20 seconds and then stood up and moved to a window overlooking the thick forest outside. A hanging fog had crept in, keeping visibility low. He calmed himself before speaking. "Are you kidding me?" he asked Noble without looking at him.

"What? It didn't come up," he spoke.

"How could it not come up?" Barnes rubbed at his forehead.

"I called and she answered the phone, 'Hi, this is Tina Walker,'" Noble said. "She didn't say, 'Hi, this is Tina Walker, wife of Senator William Walker, second-term, second-generation politician'...Come on, Brad."

"Yeah, yeah, you're right, kid." Barnes' blood pressure was returning to normal. "I just hate surprises, that's all."

"Well, it sure makes a little more sense as to why this guy felt like he deserved answers immediately," Noble mentioned.

"Wouldn't you think something like that would be in the kid's background?" Barnes said, still confused that he hadn't known Walkers' was a family of politicians.

"Does it really make that much difference?" Noble asked.

"I guess we'll know in a minute or two." Barnes could hear heavy footsteps moving across the adjacent room.

William Walker Jr. burst through the double door of the suite with all of the subtlety of a rhinoceros, Agent Wright in tow. He moved directly toward the wet bar at the back of the room and poured himself a scotch, dry. His shadow stood by his side at attention.

"Don't be upset if I don't offer you gentlemen something to drink," the senator huffed.

"No, Senator, we're fine, thanks," Barnes retorted.

"Mrs. Walker will not be joining us, I'm sorry," the senator said, leaning forward against the bar on his free hand while swilling a whisky on the rocks. He was purposely avoiding eye contact or acknowledging the detectives, trying to belittle their importance to him. "The whole affair has her completely exhausted. She's resting in our room."

"We understand, Senator, I'm sure that—" Noble started.

"Oh, you understand do you now, Detective?" the senator interrupted, finally turning toward them. "Have you ever had a loved one murdered?"

"Sir, we don't have all of the facts yet, I just—"

"What I think he's trying to say, Senator, is that we're very sorry for the loss of your son and we're doing everything we can to find out what happened out there on the beach," Barnes re-tracked.

"Yeah, I'm sure you are," Walker answered with a hint of sarcasm, turning his back on the detectives again as he refilled his drink. "Tell me everything. And since the wife is not here, don't leave out any details."

Barnes recounted the entire gruesome crime scene, as well as Doc Nichols' eyewitness account, in about 15 minutes.

"So, you're telling me that you think this whole thing is over a woman, and I wouldn't be surprised. Kid couldn't keep his prick in his pants."

"It's an avenue we're investigating at this point," the senior detective offered.

The senator nodded. "What do we know about the second casualty?"

"Percival Sutherland," Barnes offered as the senator emptied the contents of his glass down his gullet. "Does the name mean anything to you?"

"Can't say I've ever heard it. Do you know why he was there?"

"He was a bouncer at a strip club. As I stated, the doctor's account of events points to an argument over a woman, and some evidence gathered at the scene substantiates the claim. Was Mason seeing anyone you were aware of?"

"Detective, Mason and I weren't always on the best terms recently," the senator droned. "No, I'm not aware of his romantic status."

"My theory is a jealousy encounter that went very awry," Noble blurted.

"We still have a lot of investigating to do and questions we must find answers for," Barnes steadied the conversation's course.

"I understand the complexities of an investigation, I'm a United States senator, Detective." He was direct. "Gentlemen, I'm a busy man and the nation waits for no one. Politics is a dirty business and there are people out there with a hatred for our nation, my family, and our way of doing things."

"Are you intimating that this is somehow related to you?" Barnes and Noble looked at each other. "We're still investigating, Senator. If you have information that provides an alternative motive, I'll need that intel. I'm sure you want to know exactly what happened out there?"

"Of course, I want to know, he's my son!" The senator turned angry. "Part of Mason's reason for moving out here was to distance himself from our politics. I do not think this was politically driven. In fact, I think you're headed down the right path with the crime of passion avenue. And quite frankly, the sooner you can wrap this up, the better. Our family is in shock, my wife is traumatized by this loss. We need closure and I'd like to see this end quickly."

"We're not sitting on our hands here, Senator. But the investigation needs to run its course. We'll keep you posted," Barnes dug in.

"Fine, Detective. I'll give you some room to try and figure this out, but if it starts dragging, I'm going to get involved."

The senator was staunch. "And trust me, you don't want that. You have an eyewitness account. Am I making myself clear, gentlemen?"

"Crystal," Barnes answered. "But, Senator, keep out of my investigation until I have a chance to get some answers, or I assure you I'll handle things in a much different manner. I may be just a small-town cop, but if you really want to know what happened out there, you won't muddy the waters."

"Fair enough," droned the senator as he swallowed another huge gulp of whisky, his rage hidden beneath a politician's façade. "Fair enough."

CHAPTER 17

The detectives stood at the entrance of the hotel waiting for their car, but no words were exchanged. The agent assigned to Senator Walker had accompanied them through the lobby and stood watch, as he was accustomed. Barnes' phone rang and he pulled it from his sport coat. It was a number that looked familiar, but he couldn't place it.

"Barnes here," he answered, moving away from the others.

"Brad, Fairbanks here, how are you holding up?"

He almost bit his tongue…he wasn't sure how he felt about the deputy director. He must've been privy to the plea bargain that released the drunken monster who killed his wife.

"Fairbanks, I hear congratulations are in order," he replied in an undetected mock tone. "Director now, huh?"

"Nothing is concrete at this point, I'm just filling in until a permanent solution is determined." Fairbanks chuckled. "But it's nice to know you're keeping an eye on me."

"Tough to miss the big headlines. Speaking of which, the last time we talked, you were going to get me some information on the illegal who killed Patricia."

"I've got some motions in play, you know the political climate surrounding foreign sovereignty is murky at best right now. The border is a hyper-sensitive topic, as I'm certain you are aware. Being an election year, everything is cattywampus, but I promise you, if I can get to him, I will."

The response eased a bit of the detective's temperament. "Thanks, I'm not going to lie and say I'm a fan, but Patricia trusted you, so..."

"I hope to change that, Brad. I'm a big fan of Patricia's and of yours. As a matter of fact, that's why I'm calling. I understand that you have a pretty high-profile case building out there?"

"How would you know that? Why would you know that?"

"Calm down, Brad, I'm calling as a friend," Fairbanks soothed. "The son of a U.S. senator was killed. Did you somehow not believe the FBI would be notified?"

"Right. Of course. I'm sorry, I'm trying to get my arms around this thing. I just met with the senator and he's not helping," Barnes unburdened.

"I don't know too much about the senator, but I will offer this. If there is anything I can do to help you, just reach out and ask. I owe that much to Patricia. She was one of the best." Fairbanks sighed.

The old detective recalled the 'I'll always have your back' statement he'd made at the award banquet. "I may take you up on that."

"Seriously, Brad. Anything at all, don't hesitate. And good luck."

"Thanks for the reach out, Director." They both shared a light chuckle and the line clicked off. Barnes eyed his phone and shook his head in silent appreciation before returning it to his pocket.

The valet was pulling up with the car and he and Colt jumped in. Agent Wright slowly disappeared in the rearview mirror as they readied to depart the Crown Hotel. The man in black lifted his wrist toward his mouth. "They're leaving now, sir," he spoke into a miniature transmitter.

"Good," came the reply. "Is everything in place?"

Wright looked toward the valet parking garage and received a thumbs up from a man dressed as an attendant, but who did not work there. "Yes, sir, we are operational," he responded, watching the fake attendant disappear into the structure.

"You heard that hick town detective challenging me? A sitting United States senator," Winslow almost screamed into the transmitter. "I've half the mind to take him out right now."

"We need to be smart, Senator, and guide him down the path to closing this our way," Agent Wright returned. "We need to keep our cool."

"You keep your own cool and remember who you work for," the senator pounced. "He doesn't know I'm the biggest dick in the brothel yet. But I'll have my time with this little crawdad, mark my words."

✳✳✳

"Was there a reason that guy needed to walk us out?" Noble asked, looking over his shoulder as they pulled away from the curb.

Barnes flipped on the windshield wipers as they drove from underneath the canopied entrance. The gentle drizzle turned to rain and was picked up by the soft glow of lights from the overhead parking cover. "Just to make sure we left, I suppose."

Colton watched as the agent returned to the hotel. "What's with that guy anyway?"

"I wondered that also," Barnes eased the car back onto the main road, down to the coastal highway. "Kind of seemed a bit more 'bodyguard' than agent to me."

"Sometimes you scare me." Noble shook for effect. "But that is exactly what I was thinking."

Barnes' mind was busy sorting through the meeting with the senator. He'd been in more than his share of these situations and realized that, from an informational standpoint, there usually wasn't much to be gained. Emotions are high. There's tension, denial, and sometimes even misdirected anger all pulling on the family or friends at once. But this situation was a little bit different. It was more like they had taken a meeting.

"So, what did you think of the senator, Colt?" Barnes blinked, checking the mirrors.

"I think that agent was right." Colton fiddled with his shoulder strap. "He's just a kind of no-nonsense guy. He's straight to the point and matter-of-fact. Wouldn't you agree?"

Barnes thought for a second, "Yeah, I guess he is that, indeed. A very old-school type, like from a different time period guy it seemed to me."

"How's that?" Noble prompted.

"Well, for starters, does anybody really wear suspenders anymore?" He laughed. "No, I'm kidding, of course, but the comment about the wife not being there so don't hold back. Or the ridiculous over-the-top bravado, give me a break."

"Oh, there's no doubt this guy is full of himself," Colton stated. "But isn't that a politician thing? Aren't they all too big for their britches?"

Barnes had encountered them before. "Yeah, most of them—above the law and greedy as crap, too."

"So, at least we know what we're working with," the young detective reinforced. "I loved the way he tried to control the entire situation in there."

"That's what he's used to," Barnes observed. "He needs to be the guy running the show."

"How long do you think they'll be here?" Noble asked, finally relaxing into his seat.

"I think that depends." Barnes moved his toothpick around in his mouth. "They have to ID the body yet and probably go through his things at the office. They'll need to make arrangements to transport out of state and that can be complicated, even for a senator. It'll likely be another couple of days at the least."

"When are they looking at the body?" Noble watched as a huge, big rig squeezed by on the way up the mountain.

"Eugene told me they'd be there tomorrow morning." Barnes watched the taillights blaze in the rear-view mirror as he broke into the turn. "He said he'd get his eyes on the bouncer after that, might have some reports for us as early as 2:00."

Barnes wasn't anticipating anything other than the usual cause of death reports. He figured there'd just be confirmation of the cardiac arrest on Sutherland and probably Eugene would substantiate Doc Nichols' summation of rapid blood loss on the young Walker. But just in case, he asked the coroner to be extra vigilant in his review of the victims. With the latest development on Walker's family, he was glad he did...it may come in handy. The senator did not strike the veteran officer as a guy who would accept anything less.

"Should we be in attendance?" Noble asked. "You know, the senator could try and steamroll Eugene like he did to us."

"I think we'll give Senator and Mrs. Walker some space to grieve." Barnes scratched at his eyebrow. "Eugene will be okay. I'm sure it's not his first rodeo."

"You know, there is one thing I did like about the senator..." Colton smiled wide. "He seemed to be siding with me a bit on the case resolution?"

"How's that, kid?" Barnes took his eyes off the road, briefly looking at his partner.

"Well, he did say that the kid couldn't keep his prick in his pants?" Noble recounted. "That still makes the fight being over a girl that much more likely, right?"

Barnes' mind started racing. He couldn't help but show a little frustration and pounded on the steering wheel. He quickly checked the mirrors and turned up the speed on the wipers so he could get a better view out of the windshield.

"You alright?" Colt looked around as if Barnes had spotted some danger he needed to be aware of.

About two hundred yards ahead was a turnout to allow slower cars to defer to backed-up traffic. "There it is," Barnes muttered under his breath. He quickly pulled the car off the road and came to a stop. He turned toward his partner and placed his arm over the back of the seat.

"How about that?" Barnes barked. "That pompous jerk had me so pissed off at him that I didn't catch it."

"Huh?" Colt baited.

"You're a genius, kid," Barnes said. "He said his boy couldn't keep his prick in his pants. He almost said it with pride."

"Yes, that's what I recall," Noble agreed.

"Yet, this afternoon, Kayleigh tells us she practically threw herself at him at some point, but he didn't respond."

"Maybe he wasn't attracted to her that way?" Noble said.

"Kid, she told us she walked around half-naked knowing he was there, hoping to incite an interlude," Barnes said. "She was pretty, and we saw her without makeup after a day of crying. If she's dressed up and made up, I'm guessing she's reasonably attractive."

"What are you getting at?"

"How many naked girls with a body like that are you turning down?" Barnes asked pointedly.

"If I'm single?" Noble admitted. "None."

"Right," Barnes added. "My point exactly. So, why would the senator want us to think that his kid is a player?"

"He seemed kind of proud of that, actually," Noble said.

"Yeah, but he also heard you saying that you felt this was a simple jealousy killing," Barnes supposed. "At first, he was very intense about the case and how it was handled. But then he flipped the script. He was pushing, wanted the case closed fast."

"And I was giving him the out?" Noble offered.

"You were giving him the easy way out," Barnes affirmed. "He's smart. He took what we gave him and turned it into a stronger motive."

"That means the senator knows more than he's telling us," Noble realized. "Maybe there is a political angle. Something he's hiding?"

"I don't know, but I was sure there was more to this than the obvious." Barnes reset himself in the driver's seat, checked the mirrors, and pulled back out onto the road. "Gotta do some digging. There's something in the closet, maybe something in the kid's past, something that could upset his political apple cart. I'm really anxious to get my eyes on that clerk recorder's info on the kid's business in Connecticut now."

"What are you expecting?"

"Just anything that'll really give us something to sink our teeth into." Barnes stared blankly at the road.

"You're convinced this is not a simple jealousy killing?"

"My gut tells me no way, there's something else going on. We have an investigation to complete but I'm more than open to another resolution. We need to get back to the office, I want to check my email and see if we've received anything back from the Connecticut recorder's office." The car hydroplaned and drifted into the oncoming lane, narrowly missing a big hauler.

"Whoa, I'd like to make it home in one piece, Brad."

He feathered the gas and brought the Crown Victoria back to his side. "Is this rain ever going to let up?"

"Not looking like it. Hasn't rained this hard in at least 10 years."

"When I get done at the office, I'm going to head to the Nest for a drink to relax a bit. You interested?"

Noble sighed. "Been a long day, partner. I really should spend some time with Sara."

"Oh, crap. I'm sorry, meant to tell you, I met her today."

"Yeah, she texted me. She likes you."

"You married well, kid." Barnes smiled and thought of his beloved Patricia. "I understand."

It was quiet the rest of the way to the office except for the rain lashing against the windshield. Barnes parked the car near the station so he could get inside fast.

"Colt," Barnes grabbed his arm. "Let me give you some advice. You may not be able to teach an old dog new tricks, but maybe an old dog can teach you something. I gave my life to the department and I'm sitting here alone."

"Yeah?" Colton looked confused.

"Don't mess it up! Get home to Sara. I'll see you in the morning with fresh eyes."

"Thanks, Bradford."

***

Agent Wright was back upstairs in the suite. He pulled the headphones off of his head and looked at the senator. "You heard it."

"Stay close to them. This detective could be a problem. He said he was going to the Nest for a drink, right?"

"Yeah, what're you thinking?"

"Sounds like he'll be alone. I'm thinking it might be a great opportunity to communicate on a different level. Can you make the necessary arrangements?"

"Not a lot of time, but I'll see what I can do."

"Good. He's an old guy. He should understand the old ways of doing things. Send the message. Clear?"

"Clear."

"Let me know when it's done," Senator Walker ordered and then stormed out of the room to meet his wife for dinner in the hotel's steakhouse.

CHAPTER 18

Barnes dropped Colt off at home and headed into the office. There was nothing to do at the granny flat except watch TV anyway. He tossed his keys on the desk and pulled the toothpick from his mouth, then bent it in half. The wastebasket was wedged from underneath his workspace by his foot, and he flicked the gnawed splinter in. *How much worse can smoking really be?* His mind was playing tricks with him. The tired detective plopped into his uncomfortable chair—the same chair that Grimes had sat in all those years. *What am I missing here, Ben?* he asked the departed as he rested there, staring blankly at the monitor, trying to clear his mind.

The office was almost empty. At this hour on a Saturday evening, most of the department had headed home already. But Barnes didn't really have a home to go to. His mind drifted to thoughts about Patricia. He reminisced on their old college days together. All the great times they had shared. The trip they had all taken that he and Jim had talked about earlier that day. He took the mental journey through their courtship in school. Both had lived to party on the weekends. Their scholarly pursuits kept them completely segregated, buried in books and assignments until then. But they had been inseparable on those breaks. It didn't really matter what they did—hiking or camping or a whole lot of partying—as long as they were together.

The romance blossomed, and two years after Patricia graduated, they were married. It was a small ceremony on the beach in Santa Barbara, just a quaint gathering with family and friends. He remembered how beautiful she looked that day. The way her pale blue eyes sparkled in the afternoon sunlight, the gold flecks glowing when she smiled. They had stood there under the gazebo, hand in hand. He just stared into those eyes so deeply that he hadn't even heard the pastor's cues in the exchange of vows. That brought a chuckle from the gallery, but his beautiful wife just beamed, happy.

They moved to L.A. the next year where they both accepted jobs—Bradford as a junior detective with the LAPD and Patricia as a field officer with the FBI. It was a grueling schedule and a steep learning curve for them both. But they were committed to their work and to each other. Every night together was like a complete reset. She knew how to relax him and help him purge. He knew how to make her smile and listen without trying to fix anything. Neither cared how they spent the time, it was the company of the other that each one craved.

Then he moved on to that last night together. The awards banquet in her honor. She was so happy, so confident and comfortable. He recalled how she worked the room, made it about everyone else and not herself. How she found happiness in the success of others, of her team. He remembered how she smiled at him when the director gave her the award—not at anyone else in the party but at him. He missed that smile.

He flashed to the scene of the accident…the smoky interior of the car, her bleeding, broken speech, trying to talk her into fighting. They pulled her out and lay her right on the street. The paramedics worked feverishly, compressing her chest and monitoring her vitals, but they wouldn't let him get close. He was a wreck, his shirt was drenched in her blood, his dislocated right arm hung at his side, and his tuxedo shirt torn from being pulled out of the mangled steel of the Rover.

His heart pounded in his chest and his hands balled into fists as he looked over at the heavily tattooed Latino man being handcuffed after being pulled out of the dump truck and blowing a 1.9 bac test. He wanted to talk to him, ask him what had happened, but he knew that if he got close, he'd pummel him to within a fraction of his life.

He was destroyed when the prosecutor plea bargained the trial that saw the driver responsible for killing his wife deported and sent to Mexico, never to be seen or heard from again. He was emotionally ill-equipped to continue working and took a leave of absence, grateful that his buddy, Jimmy, had reached out and dragged him to Rocky Point.

Filling in for Grimes he hadn't counted on, but in reality, the work kept him from doing the very thing that he was doing now—pining away and getting depressed. He sat back up straight and tapped the spacebar on his computer, 'waking' it up.

His inbox was filled with the usual interdepartmental communications. He began filing them away when the email from the county recorder in Avon, Connecticut scrolled onto the screen. He double-clicked it and a slew of .pdf attachments packed the screen.

"Hope this helps, if you have any other questions, just drop me a note," read the body of the electronic message. "Do me a favor though and send some of that lovely California weather out our way, ha-ha."

"If he only knew," Barnes scoffed, listening to the rain beat on the roof of the empty office. He opened the first .pdf, which was just a copy of the business license. The second file contained a much bigger document with financial information, including taxes, and confirmed Barnes' suspicions on why a successful business would be closed down. His mind was processing. *Again, why would he close a lucrative practice?* he questioned. *It takes a while to build clientele. And what happens to those patients when an office closes?*

Energy reserves started to kick in as he continued to open files and scan through the information. Everything in those files pointed to a legitimate and successful business. There were no city complaints, no leans or unpaid rents, and no fines of any kind. He read through a couple of documents that he printed out as he sat there at his desk, sipping from his third cup of coffee.

What are you doing in California, Mason? he ruminated, shuffling those papers around. *Why would you leave that practice behind?*

He hadn't thought to ask the senator or his wife, yet. It was too soon to be questioning them, but he knew that, eventually, he would have to. He was still considering the issue when the computer 'dinged' and another email populated the inbox. He became instantly curious when the sender's name came up as 'USER'@Connpublib.edu. Two mouse clicks later and the window expanded, providing only a couple of hypertext links and a quick blurb; 'still waters run deep'.

Barnes paused for a moment, considering his options. It could be some sort of e-bomb that could wreak havoc on the network, but he knew the department's cyber security was strong. If it had been any other address, he might've passed it over, but the Connecticut public library address made the link too compelling to ignore.

He hovered over the hypertext for just a second before activating the link. Another tab was initialized in his browser and the page began slowly loading. The header was 'Hartford Courant' displayed in bold English text. Barnes could see that this was a local Connecticut newspaper site. An arrow pointing to the bottom part of the page found Barnes scrolling down to read the byline: SENATORS SON NOT SINGING. The detective chuckled at the Credence Clearwater reference, but the article was anything but humorous.

Connecticut (AP/UPI) – Mason Wells Walker declined to take the stand in court today in response to questioning surrounding allegations of business misconduct, sexual harassment, and statutory rape. Senator William Wallace Walker Jr. (D) sat quietly while his son avoided testifying in his own defense. The prosecution team, visibly upset over the missed opportunity to cross-examine the accused, called attention to the victims' families—many of whom wept uncontrollably in the large courtroom. In particular, the members of the Grayson family, whose daughter, Amanda, has been missing since the filing of the case last September.

Walker, whose practice thrived helping young women and men who had been victims of abuse, neglect, and drug or alcohol addiction, came under fire when Grayson allegedly informed her parents of the inappropriate conduct of the therapist. Mrs. Grayson launched a campaign against her daughter's mental health physician, taking out ad space and hanging fliers throughout the county that said: Walker is not a therapist, but instead, 'the rapist'.

Walker claims that he began treating the young Amanda, who had turned to drugs because the home environment was volatile due to her mother's alcohol and anger challenges. He has denied all accusations as unfounded and ridiculous attempts to smear his family's political agenda.

Grayson claimed that instead of providing proper therapy, he brainwashed her and turned her against her own family.

In a civil suit, Mason Walker is going after the Grayson's and one other family over the defamation that forced the closure of his practice and destroyed his career.

Senator Walker spoke briefly to the media following the proceedings with his arms over his son's shoulders in a show of support:

"Anyone with 20/20 vision can clearly see that these charges have been trumped up by a desperate woman. This woman's own instability and addiction problems have destroyed her family and driven her young daughter away. If these accusations are to have any merit whatsoever, it must be factored in that the Grayson's were delinquent in therapy payments to the tune of four months, and Amanda will have to step forward and substantiate these claims. But she won't. The embarrassment and humiliation caused by her mother must be overwhelming for her. We wish Amanda and her family and friends reconciliation and happiness. The

Walkers have served the great state of Connecticut for over 50 years, and we will continue to do so into the future. Thank you all for your support in these tough times."

The judge will review the case and present his verdict after the weekend unless something changes. It's unlikely that without Amanda's testimony, Walker will be found guilty. And with the political pressure that a grandstanding senator can muster, I'd be surprised if the decision to dismiss the case has not already been made.

The byline was Martin Bender. The detective made a note about contacting him.

He had his answer now for a couple of key questions. It was time to get that cold drink and relax a little with his thoughts.

CHAPTER 19

The relentless storm continued to pound the town with rain and wind that gusted like a hurricane, turning the short drive from the station house to the Nest into a challenge. He sloshed the Crown Victoria into a parking stall near the rear entrance and sprinted to the door to avoid getting drenched. Seconds later, he plopped into his usual seat at the end of the bar.

"You look like you could use a tall one, Detective."

"That's affirmative, thanks, Matt."

Barnes sipped at the beer slowly, mulling the new communication, applying it to what they already had on the senator's son. He quickly understood the senator's odd behavior and knew he was hiding this and maybe even more. With a sharp tingle, he also realized his bladder could no longer contain the three cups of coffee he devoured while sitting in front of the computer, so he needed relief.

He still had a paper towel in his hand when he opened the door. The moment he stepped out of the restroom, he sensed something was amiss. He scanned the hallway and quickly found that his favored seat at the end of the bar had been taken. He'd left it only moments ago. Now a mammoth mountain of a man, wearing all black under a denim biker vest, sat there. His thick, wiry beard was covered with the foam from the detective's beer.

Against his better judgment, he was about to confront the big gentleman. But when he reached the end of the corridor leading back into the Crow's Nest, he noticed four more men, all of similar size and appearance, scattered throughout the pub.

He cursed himself for leaving his Glock in the car. But after a full day in that holster, he couldn't wait to get it off—a mistake he vowed not to make again. He looked over his shoulder back down the hallway in case beating a hasty retreat became necessary. He realized the avenue might not be available when another gigantic man with a crowbar in his hands moved into position at the rear door. He really wished that Noble would've taken him up on that offer for a drink after work.

The normally bustling pub was already having a slower than typical night because of the inclement weather. It was painfully obvious that these out-of-place and unwelcome visitors had caused significant unrest. The few remaining patrons migrating toward a quick exit told that story.

Behind the bar, Matt exchanged a very uncomfortable look with the confused Barnes. The bartender glanced down to where he kept the baseball bat he had once levied at the detective and the councilman in jest. Barnes nodded in understanding.

Taking a deep breath, he slipped onto the barstool next to the behemoth who had stolen his seat. Barnes was overcome with the smell of bacon and body odor on the man as if he'd been in the same clothes for a week. Dark, dirty hair covered his arms all the way up over his sleeveless shoulders, covering a litany of prison-cut tattoos. Stretched to its limit, a black bandana barely made it around the huge skull it covered.

"Well, I'd offer to buy you a beer..." Barnes said casually. "But I think I already did."

"Oh, was that yours?" the man burped. "It was just sitting on the bar when I got here, so I figured it was a free for all."

"No harm done, big boy. I'll tell you what." Barnes smiled, confident. "How about I buy you and your friends a round and we call it good for the night? There's no one here to keep the place open for, anyway."

"My friends?" questioned the man before swallowing the last of the detective's beer.

"Yes," Barnes chuckled. "You know, the other four impeccably attired gentlemen who look just like you?"

The giant creature leaned back on the stool and peered around the detective. "Them guys? I don't know them. I'm just here to soak up some local flavor."

"Soak up some flavor, huh?" Barnes echoed before turning toward the interior of the room. "Hey, guys, your buddy here wants to know what kind of beer you want. The next round is on him, he says."

They looked at each other, stupefied. Then, all at once, they shouted back, "Right on, Mike!"

"Make it a pitcher for me, bro!"

"Ox rocks!"

"They certainly seem to know you…um, Ox, is it?" the detective chuckled.

The gigantic man just stared forward with a dumb smile on his face. "I don't know. Maybe I seen 'em before."

Barnes went to reach into his coat, but the big man grabbed his arm with a heavy paw. The detective relaxed and slowly opened his lapel with his free hand. Seeing no weapon, the monster released his grip. Barnes pulled out his emergency cigarette and eyed it as if it was the winning lotto ticket. He ran the length of it under his nostrils, breathing in the dank aroma, and closed his eyes in ecstasy.

"You can't smoke that in here," Ox slurred. "It's illegal."

"Oh, you don't have to tell me that." Barnes smirked. "I'm a cop."

The look on Ox's face was blank.

Barnes scratched a match on the countertop and lit the thin tobacco tube. "Oh, they didn't tell you that, I see?" Barnes looked at Ox.

"I don't know what you're talking about." Ox steadied himself. "Don't matter anyway, money's money."

Barnes' smile suddenly grew wide. "Probably doesn't matter that we come in pairs then, either, does it?"

The back door to the pub swung open, and Colton stepped in over the fleshy heap who was guarding the exit.

"Hey, partner!" he yelled. "I felt a little guilty about skipping out on you tonight. But then I get here and you're having a party without me?"

"How did you get in here?" Ox asked, looking over his shoulder and down the hallway. "We're closed."

"Oh, that's what your buddy must have been trying to say while he was gurgling teeth and blood?" Noble shrugged. "I guess I couldn't understand him."

"You mother f—" Ox said, standing up and moving toward the younger cop.

Barnes knew it was time and flicked his lit cigarette into the monster's beard. He panicked for just an instant. It was just long enough.

"MATT!" Barnes yelled out.

The bartender answered the call and tossed the bat toward the anxious detective. In a second, he had plucked it out of the air, spun 270 degrees, generating as much force as he could, and took aim at the bewildered thug. He landed a direct blow that found his temple and stopped him cold in his spot. Two more quick cracks on the noggin' and the giant was out for the night.

Noble reached across the bar and grabbed two beer bottles. He broke them on the solid wood counter, converting them into sharp, jagged-edged weapons.

The four other paid henchmen took positions surrounding the detectives. Flanking them against the bar, they began to close in with knives drawn.

"Matt, get down and stay down!" Barnes yelled just as a mug flew past his ear and shattered the big mirror on the wall behind the surprised bartender.

Noble quickly moved to his left to split the attackers apart. He didn't wait for an assault move. He lunged at the bigger of the two men in front of him, who began viciously slashing at him as he came. Colt was quicker, though, and caught his assailant's arm with a bottle. To avoid being stabbed, he stepped quickly to his right. The bottle broke off and left two shards deep in his attacker's shoulder. Blood instantly started to flow and he screamed in agony. As he tried to remove the painful glass, Noble slammed his knee with a sidekick that buckled him to the ground.

The other biker jumped on his back and tried to get his arms around Colt's neck. But the young detective anticipated the move and gave a furious reverse head butt, breaking the man's nose instantly. He recoiled, wiping the blood from his eyes, and Noble spun and caught him with an uppercut to the solar plexus. The second man went down, too, gasping for air. Noble quickly cuffed one arm from each man over the metal footrest along the bottom of the counter.

Then he turned to help his partner just in time to see his two attackers headed out the back exit. On the run, one of the men was holding his dangling forearm. Barnes had broken it with the bat when he stabbed at him. After seeing the bone protrude through the skin, he and his partner had double-timed it out of there, picking up the guard at the back entrance along the way.

"You wanna put the call in while I get this group ready for transport?" Barnes checked himself for any injuries and pointed to Colt when he noticed the blood on his partner's arm.

"Wow, I didn't even feel it."

Matt caught on and tossed him a towel.

"Great thinking, Matt, I'd forgotten about the bat." Barnes winked. "We might not have made it out of here without your help. Thanks."

Matt could scarcely even respond—his adrenaline was still pumping through his veins. "Oh, yeah, I was just, ah, no problem…"

Noble finished wrapping the towel around his arm. "Matt, can I use your phone? Matt?"

"Huh? Oh, yeah, sure…here you go." He put the phone on the counter, hands still shaking. "Would you guys mind if I asked you to do me a favor though?"

"Of course, Matt." Barnes asked, "What is it? Do you need us to explain this to the owner?"

The bartender leaned against the counter, his legs weakening. "Would you mind going to one of the other pubs in town the next time you're thirsty?"

Barnes couldn't help but laugh. "You know what this means, Colt?"

Noble put the receiver between his shoulder and his ear and squeezed the towel on the wound. "Yeah, we're getting too close to something or somebody. You were probably right about the senator."

CHAPTER 20

The next morning came far too fast. If it hadn't been for the strong odor of rich coffee filling the small office area, Barnes might've been upset. Instead, he nursed the warm brew while eyeballing the crime board Noble had put together. A scan of Corrina's picture had been added, the locations of the therapist's office and Lovergirls, and a slew of sticky notes with hints and ideas scratched in red pen.

What are we walking into? Whose party are we crashing? Frustration oozed like cheese through a grater in the grey-haired detective's mind. He wanted answers but knew that, oftentimes, it was just better to push forward, and the answers would come. He thought he heard Patricia's voice, *Stay the course.*

Colton exploded into the room.

"They aren't talking, partner, just like you said. I thought that Ox guy's head was big before. You should see it now after the lumps you left with that bat." Colt laughed as he returned to his desk from the holding cell.

"I didn't figure they would. I put a call out to the local hospitals and clinics but the guy with the fracture will probably keep it underground."

"So, what was that? Were they actually planning on killing a cop?"

"No, they were probably just supposed to send a message," Barnes ruminated. "Intended to scare us off the trail."

"You scared?"

"Nope, just pissed off."

"What next?" Noble tried to make eye contact.

"Let's ask ourselves some logical questions. If you're going to send in some muscle then there's something at stake, right?

"That would seem to make sense," Noble agreed.

"And if these guys are not willing to talk, even with reduced charges on the table, then..."

"They're scared."

Barnes scratched at the facial hair. "Yeah, or loyal. With this group, I'll take scared, which means whoever is giving orders has power or influence."

"Are you thinking the senator again? We already talked about that?"

"Funny that you mention it. That paperwork on the therapist's business in Connecticut came in last night. Some interesting stuff."

"How's that?"

"The kid was on trial for some pretty heinous accusations... allegations of rape, misconduct, you name it." Barnes was almost flippant.

"But the background was clean..."

Barnes smiled like the Cheshire cat. "How do you suppose something like that happens?"

Noble stared back at his partner.

"Wait for it..."

Colton's head drooped. "The senator..."

"That's what I'm thinking. Who else could pull those kinds of strings?"

"Partner?"

"I'm not sure what it is yet, but there's something big hiding in the shadows."

"I don't know, Brad...I'm not the one with experience here, but if the senator was trying to guide us to an easy conclusion on this, wouldn't sending a message be a mistake?"

"Yeah, unless something changed or he's getting inside intel."

"Don't look at me, I was in the bar with you, remember?"

Barnes coughed into his hand. "Not what I was thinking, kid, but we need more data. We keep digging. Let's see what we can cull from Lovergirls and find out what Eugene and the coroner's office can offer."

"What are we after?"

"Nothing specific at this point but information. Let's get over to the hall and pick up that second warrant and head out to the strip club, see what we can find out about Sutherland. After that, we'll head over to the doc's and check in on him. Maybe see if there's anything else he remembers."

"Roger that." Noble opened and shut his jaw, clicking his teeth. "You're not thinking the doc is involved...are you?"

"That's highly unlikely, but we can't rule anything out at this point."

"No, I guess not, but the guy's old as dirt."

"Truth is, when people are in shock, they don't always remember things clearly. I'm just thinking it will be good to go over the incident again, maybe something shook loose in his subconscious." Barnes glanced at the board once more. "Of course, we want to make sure he's okay, too."

CHAPTER 21

The smell of a nightclub didn't seem to differ much from joint to joint and this place was no exception. Maybe it was the buildup of spilled alcohol with the hint of vomit stomped into musty shag carpeting over the years. Perhaps it was the palpable blend of personal fragrances dusted over sweat, fused together with cigarettes in a rigorously climate-controlled environment. Whatever the case, Barnes knew with familiarity that they had arrived in the dive known as Lovergirls.

He flashed his badge and announced to the bartender that they wished to speak to the manager or owner, whoever might be resident. Without really even acknowledging them, he picked up an old-style phone and punched a few digits on the keypad. "Cops are here," he said, turning his head away from the detectives. "How should I know? They didn't say and I didn't ask," he spat into the phone intensely.

An ape of a man stood near the entrance of the club dressed in black from head to toe, wearing a shirt that read security on the front and back. It was at least one size too small, and the flak jacket and other protective wear were easily traceable under the strained fabric.

"Hey, 'G,'" yelled the bartender. "Can you take these guys up to the den? Lickety-split please, the night crowd is picking their way in and will get spooked if we gotta couple of detectives hanging around."

Though he was more rotund in appearance than fit, he was a heap of muscle. "Sure thing," he answered. "Gentlemen, if you'll follow me?"

The place was laid out like a dinner theater with seats and small tables in the pit area surrounding a short runway with a large deck at its end and a pole that stretched to the ceiling. Behind them, a couple of steps up were larger tables and booths. A couple of steps more was the next level with some counters that faced the stages, and behind that was the long-curved bar. Mosaic balls hung from the ceiling deflecting lights all over the room. The entire place was lined with walls of mirrors so that every patron could get a view of the action. Music boomed throughout the hall, reverberating off of the hard floors like an echo chamber.

With the body of a refrigerator and the mentality of a linebacker, 'G' led them through the pit, past the stages, and to the back of the club. They walked up a small ramp and through some curtains into the dressing area. There were a couple of girls getting ready to go on—one whose exceptional figure and stealthy chest caused both of the detectives to sneak a peek. She noticed and winked as they passed by. They entered a hallway and plodded up a staircase that switched back until reaching a large red-painted door with a large peephole.

The huge security guard knocked twice, waited, and then twice again. A few seconds later, the door opened and a woman in her early 40s smiled, inhaling the smoke from a long, thin cigarette, and exhaling it towards the ceiling. As the billowing smoke cleared, Barnes was quick to notice that tobacco and alcohol had conspicuously taken their toll on the woman and she appeared at least 10 years older than she probably was.

Dressed in a loose-fitting blouse that did little to hide her oversized and obviously enhanced breasts, she turned and flaunted a pair of zebra shorts that were riding far too high. Remarkably, she had the legs of a 25-year-old. Her blonde hair had been matted out in an attempt to hide the horrible hair extensions that fell as far as her waistline.

"Hello, boys, and what brings you to our little club? You're not looking for a 'special', I trust?" she cooed, holding her hand out as if she was royalty, expecting it to be kissed. "I'm Sable, I own the place. Come in." She turned and strutted into the room.

"No, ma'am, no special or anything. We're looking for information on a gentleman," Barnes said.

"Detective, a whole lot of gentlemen pass through here." She smiled wryly. "What makes you think that I can help you?"

"This one worked here." Barnes watched as Sable fell into a huge circular suede sofa, set around a big heart-shaped coffee table.

Her eyes blinked hard enough that they almost caused the thick mascara eyelashes to fall off. "Oh?" she asked. "Please, gentlemen, sit down, you're making me nervous. 'G', I'll be fine. Thank you, honey." She dismissed the security guard and waited until the door closed behind the behemoth. Her demeanor seemed to change instantly. "How can I help you?"

"Does the name Percival Sutherland ring a bell?" Noble asked, watching her reaction intently.

"Percy? Oh, yes, of course. You had me frightened there for a minute." She calmed. "Percy is one of the last of an old breed. He's been with me for quite some time now. And he's truly one of the good guys."

Barnes was busy scribbling in the notepad he pulled out. "Good guys, Ms. Sable?"

"Oh, yes, I've had security people come and go, and most of them aren't worth a penny of pay. They come here looking for work and end up being nothing but trouble, chasing my girls or pedaling dope. The temptations are many here, officers," she said, crossing her legs over in a very provocative manner, exposing her crotch partially while watching the detectives as she did so.

"Yes, um, Percival, ma'am?" Noble redirected.

"Percy actually gave a shit," she said, lifting a Martini to her lips. "He gave a shit about the club and about the people. When Percy was around, nobody messed with my girls. And I mean nobody. You can ask the guy he busted up in here a year or two ago. You've got a report on that I'm certain"

"Yes, ma'am?" Barnes listened.

"But he hasn't been around for at least a month now. He picked up his last paycheck a couple of weeks ago, gave me a hug, and thanked me for letting him work here." She sat pensively. "He said he had something to do, somewhere to go...or something like that. Please tell me he's not involved with something illicit. Please, tell me?"

Barnes looked at his partner before turning back to Ms. Sable. "I'm afraid to tell you that Mr. Sutherland is deceased."

It was like an implosion. She gasped in a roomful of air, her hands rose to her face, and she convulsed before standing up and yelling out, "NO! No, no, no! This was a good man. He wasn't nefarious. You're kidding me, right? Tell me this is a joke? It has to be a joke." She moved to the curtains at the back of the room, which covered a tremendous one-way mirrored window. Pulling them slightly apart, she monitored the activity below and sulked. "How? Why? What happened?"

Barnes got up off of the couch and stood with his hands in his pockets. "Well, there was an altercation down at the beach a few days ago and two men were killed. At this point, it appears to be an argument over a woman. We thought you might help us to determine—"

Barnes was cut off by an uproarious laugh, a deep haughty bellow. "Okay, now I know you're joking. Who put you up to this? Percy, are you out there?" she yelled toward the door. "Where'd you get those badges? You pricks. That was not even funny, jerks."

"Ma'am?" Noble questioned. "This isn't exactly the reaction—"

"So, come on now, you can't be serious? You're not joking. And this was your best detective work?" She shook her head sarcastically.

"Ms. Sable, if you could share with us the names of any women who he may have been seeing or had relations with?" Noble asked.

Barnes slapped his hand on his forehead.

She took another long drag on her cigarette. "Percy was gay, boys. Percy was gay as gay," she said, blowing the smoke toward the younger detective. "Whatever happened out there did not happen over a woman, I can assure you of that."

***

"Well, that takes my simple theory of an argument over a woman out of the equation. No jealousy revenge here," Noble admitted as they walked out of the club and headed toward their cars.

The thought hadn't even occurred to Barnes. "People can go both ways, Colt."

"Yeah, but you heard her. It didn't sound to me like he had any interest in women."

"Maybe it wasn't necessarily a love triangle, but a girl could still be at the heart of it. You heard how she said he protected these girls."

"I suppose."

"Let's scavenge around the office and see if we can dredge up any reports on the altercation Ms. Sable referenced that involved Sutherland. Never know what we might find."

"I'll get on it first thing."

CHAPTER 22

"Hey, Barnsie," Colt rushed into the room, waving a file folder in his hand. "I found that incident you were looking for on the bouncer."

"That's great, the coroner just called," Barnes said, motioning to Colton for the info. "He said he was sending over some photographs for us to look at but wouldn't tell me what they were."

"What's with the mystery?" Colton shook his head in frustration. "Heart attack and a fatal stabbing, right?"

"I don't know," Barnes said, reaching for the report. "Are you going to give me that or not?"

"Well, I haven't had a chance to look at it yet." Colton pulled it away.

"Alright, have it your way." Barnes threw his hands in the air. "I'm going to get a cup of coffee while we wait for Eugene's email, or maybe he's walking them over. How long can it take to press 'send'?"

"I'll follow you then," Colton said, opening the file and beginning to read. "It's an incident report from an altercation at Lovergirls, of course. It says this happened a couple of years ago."

Barnes grabbed a Styrofoam cup. "Don't we usually give a free pass to security?"

"Well, as long as proper procedures were followed, yeah, we do." Colton flipped the pages.

"So, what happened here that was so different?" Barnes questioned, filling his cup with the afternoon dose of caffeine.

"Sutherland busted this guy up pretty good," Noble continued. "Broken jaw, broken nose, fractured eye socket, and apparently, this guy nearly lost a testicle." Colton winced at the thought.

"Well, once again, I'm feeling fairly confident that this Sutherland cat was the aggressor down on the beach, right?" Barnes filled his cup up and then headed over to his computer to check his email again.

"There are no less than four eyewitness reports that this guy got what he deserved from the bouncer," Colton noted, his lips moving as he began to read them.

"You going to tell me what happened, or should I just guess?" Barnes circled his mouse and logged on.

"Can you give me just a second or two? There's a lot to read in here, you know?" Noble quipped.

"Maybe I should send you to Evelyn Wood," Barnes retorted.

"Who the heck is Evelyn Wood, you cranky old prick?" Colton looked up from the report.

"Never mind, kid. Just keep reading, will you?" Barnes was growing impatient. "Let me know if you find something important."

Noble quickly scanned through the eyewitness accounts of the event between Sutherland and the Lovergirls patron. "Brad, all four of these folks agree that Sutherland was not out of line. It seems that this guy was manhandling one of the dancers."

"Guys are always trying to get a cheap feel." Barnes clicked his email open. "That's what guys do."

Colton read some more. "This wasn't cheap feel stuff, Brad. This guy was brutally trying to force a sexual act. Apparently, he was pulling at her hair and pushing her face into his lap, calling her names, and ignoring her pleas to stop. One guy says this creep even slapped her around."

"What are you telling me?" Barnes scrolled through his emails, anxious to see what the coroner was so tight-lipped about. "Sutherland is really a warrior for good? Is that it?"

"Well, it fits the picture the strip club manager painted and I imagine if I was the girl, I might feel that way." Colton flipped back a few more pages. "If I was this...ah, what's the girl's name? It's got to be in here somewhere."

"What girl's name, the dancer?" Barnes tapped on his mouse. "She would've filed a report, too."

"Yeah, yeah. Here it is right..." Colton paused after reading and then blurted out, "You're not going to believe this, Brad."

Barnes' frustration was already peaking. "Aw, come on now. Not you too. Can you just get to the point, kid?"

Noble set the folder on Barnes' keyboard.

"I'm trying to get something done around here, can you just tell me?"

Noble just looked at his partner and then back at the file folder.

Barnes stood straight and eyed his partner. "Okay, what am I looking for since you've obviously lost the ability to communicate?" he said, grabbing the fistful of papers.

"The name of the dancer who was involved in the altercation," Noble answered, folding his arms. "Halfway down the page, I underlined it. And there's a picture too."

Barnes' eyes widened. He looked up at his partner while processing the information. "Are you freaking kidding me? Is this the same girl? Is this Doc's wife?"

"Yes, Corrina Quinn is now Corrina Nichols," Noble clarified.

"Well, paint my britches pink and call me Nancy." Barnes was still dumbfounded. "Does the doc know her past?"

"I can't answer that, but you have to admit, this is a strange coincidence, isn't it?" Noble looked at Barnes.

"It has to be more than that," Barnes' mind was racing. "We've got two dead guys at the beach. One is her therapist and the other a bouncer where she used to work." Barnes started to pace. "And of course, the doc just happens to be there at the same time these guys kill each other? No, we just have to connect the dots."

"Anything jumping out at you?" Noble watched Barnes pace in front of the computer.

"The big thing jumping out at me right now is my blood pressure," Barnes barked at the terminal. "It can't be that hard to send a frigging email, Eugene. Even I can do it."

CHAPTER 23

Colton struggled to contain himself, but Barnes noticed the snickering.

"What's so funny, huh?" Barnes stared at him. "I'm glad that you find such humor in my agitation."

"How can I not? I've got gramps on one end at the coroner's office and 'older than dirt' right in front of me trying to navigate the complex challenges of the sophisticated tech called email." Colton laughed. "I'm surprised you can work a TV remote."

Just as he was about to let Colt have it, the computer dinged. "Ha! You see, I've got this," Barnes razzed.

"Yeah, it was probably all of the pacing you did that got it here." Noble rolled his eyes.

Barnes was fixed intently on the computer screen. "Alright, Geno, what have you got for us today?" he said to himself. "What was it that you couldn't just tell us on the phone?"

"Well, what is it? What did he find?" Noble started toward the computer.

Barnes clicked on the attachments, and they began downloading. There was a blue hyperlink on the email that Barnes had been ignoring.

Noble peeked at the screen. "Eugene wants us to Skype him when we get this downloaded."

"Skype what? What're you talking about?" Barnes looked confused having resisted the tech of social media in preference of what worked for him. "Skype this."

"Every computer here has a profile, Brad. Just click the blue link there." Noble pointed.

Barnes clicked the link and about four seconds later, Eugene's image appeared on his monitor. Barnes looked at Noble and raised an eyebrow, "Fascinating," he said, figuring the reference would be lost on his younger partner.

"Yeah, real Star Trek stuff, right?" Noble responded. "Eugene, give Brad a minute to catch up. He's a little shell-shocked right now. What are we looking at?"

"Alright, this guy is inked up pretty good so it's kind of tough to show you what's going on here," Eugene spoke in a slow, deliberate manner. "You can see the entry point of the knife in his chest in the third image. For a freak accident, this thing found about the most direct path to terminate this guy."

"What do you mean?" Barnes asked.

"Well, if you look closely just under the ribcage where it entered you'll see the jagged tear in the skin. It must've been a crude knife but the angle is steep enough to cut straight into the guy's heart without any obstruction. Have you found the weapon?"

"Still sifting," Colt blinked.

"Wait a minute. Are you saying that this wasn't an accident?" Barnes smacked his lips.

"Actually, quite the contrary," the coroner responded. "In a fight situation, the chances of landing a blow this precise are remote. There would just be too much movement. If the therapist struck first, there's no way that this guy would've been able to respond. He'd have been completely incapacitated, not to mention this guy's nose is broken. See image four."

"Was the break fresh?" Barnes asked.

"There's no doubt that the break occurred at the time of death," Eugene stated.

"So, you agree that he initiated the attack?" Noble asked.

"As I said, if this wound would have occurred first, it would have been fatal. He would not have been able to continue. So, unless there was someone else there, yes." Eugene fiddled with his prescription glasses. "If I were to draw this up, I'd say they knew each other. I think by the nature of the wounds, this guy stabbed the therapist but was caught off guard by a blow to the face that broke his nose. He probably stumbled over the bluff, and not seeing too well, tripped and went down on the knife. That's just a guess, of course."

"That's a long haul to get to a conclusion, don't you think?" Barnes asked.

"Maybe, it's your job to figure that part out. That's not why I wanted to get these images to you," Eugene said.

"Oh, but wait, there's more," Noble mocked a cheap television commercial advertisement.

Barnes looked over his shoulder at the new detective, "Really?"

"Seemed appropriate," Colt pointed back at the monitor.

"Open up image seven." Geno looked nervously around his office. "It should be a full-screen image of the torso."

Noble reached in and clicked the mouse, opening the picture. "Got it."

"Good," Eugene began. "As you can see, almost every part of this guy's upper body is covered in tattoos." A beautiful scene of exquisitely inked coy fish swam intertwined from neckline to waist.

"Are tattoos really that uncommon anymore?" Noble quizzed, squinting at the screen.

"No, of course not," Eugene responded. "But tell me what you see."

Noble was the first to answer. "Uh, I see a bunch of fish, brightly colored fish. It's nice, but it's just fish."

"Barnes? Can you see anything different?" the coroner inquired.

"I've gotta be honest, Eugene, I just see a bunch of fish and a painted chain around his neck," Barnes replied, eyeing the photo with intensity.

"Okay, that's fair," Eugene said, adjusting his glasses. "To be honest, that's how I saw it at first, too. But with all of the colors and the fish squeezed in there with lily pads, it reminded me of a 'Where's Waldo' kind of puzzle. Do you remember those?"

"Where's who?" Noble laughed.

"It's an old visual quest where you have to find the…ah, never mind, Colt." Barnes sighed. "What are you saying, Eugene?"

"Look again, Barnes," Eugene prodded. "Start with the chain around his neck."

"Why the chain?" Noble asked.

Barnes chimed in before the coroner could, "Because it's the only thing that doesn't belong in the picture."

"Right, Detective," Eugene said.

"Okay, so he's got a chain around his neck and some fish swimming on his body." Noble was becoming impatient. "Can we cut to the chase here?"

"And spoil all of the fun?" Eugene answered.

Barnes looked at the chain as it wove its way around the fish. Then he noticed something. "The chain is broken. It looks like one side is recoiling as if it snapped or broke."

"And now the fun begins." The coroner moved his face closer to the camera and smiled wide.

"Please don't do that, Eugene. I can see the hairs in your nostrils," Colton remarked, growing tired of the game.

"So, what would have been on the end of the chain, huh? Is that it, Eugene?" Barnes asked.

"That is it, precisely, Detectives," he answered, rubbing at his nose.

"Alright, a cross, a pendant." Barnes began scanning the tattoo sea.

"No, that's an army chain." Colton couldn't help but get pulled back in and stood back in front of the monitor. "We're looking for dog tags."

"Very good, Colton," the coroner said. "I thought you didn't care about Waldo?"

"Guys, can we focus please?" Barnes said, twisting his head and looking at the photo.

"Hit the control key and pull the mouse wheel, Brad," Noble suggested. The image on the screen got larger with each turn of the wheel.

"Are you kidding me?" Barnes laughed. "That's one of the reasons I hate these things. There's always something that you just don't know about them."

"Right there, Barnes," Noble indicated, pointing at two fish near his left armpit. "They're fighting over it. It's in their mouths."

"Good eyes, Detective. Zoom in a little more and you'll get the grand prize." Eugene stood back and folded his arms.

"I can read the whole thing," Barnes said. "Bingo!"

"Bingo, what?" Noble asked, looking confused.

"We might have just gotten a break, kid." Barnes slapped the desktop. "Eugene, you're a fricking genius."

"Uh, guys? So, the guy has a tattoo of dog tags being eaten by a fish and we're all dancing?" Noble scratched his head.

"We could only track this guy back a couple of years, right, Colt?" Barnes asked.

"Right," Noble answered.

"He's military. I'll run these tag numbers to a buddy of mine in L.A. and that will tell us who this bouncer really is." Barnes was copying the tag ID. "My guess is Sutherland isn't even his name. What he was doing here and who he is might just blow this whole thing open wide."

"This is getting a little confusing, partner."

"Maybe, but I feel like we're finally making some headway. While we wait for these tags to be run, let's get out and visit the doc in the morning. I'd really like to see what he's got to say about his wife and the connection to Lovergirls or Sutherland. Gut tells me he's connected to this. Not sure how deep, but with this info and the precision of the knife wound he's made the suspect list for certain."

CHAPTER 24

A fter spending the rest of the day requesting background
info, searching records, and following up on evidence
checks, Barnes left the station house at the end of his shift,
exhausted but prepared for the morning visit with Nichols.

He'd poured over the entire caseload of paperwork again,
read all of his email files, revisited all the case photos, and
allowed his subconscious to ruminate on the information. He
was hoping something would break free, bounce off his cranial
walls, and provide some new direction. He was certain there
was something he was missing, something floating in the air if
he could only reach out and grab it. He needed to connect the
dots. He needed more time to process.

Sometimes driving was where he did his best thinking. So,
instead of heading home, he took the long route and drove
along the coast, past the beach, past the diner, and turned up
Canyon Road, into the dark of night.

*Maybe Colt was right that morning on the beach. It made
little sense that Corrina would check out. Unless maybe there was
more to her past? He pondered. He'd have to look deeper, see if
anything was hiding there. And why couldn't they find out more*

about who this Sutherland guy was? Only two years of history? Just didn't ring right.

He knew he couldn't ask them. They were gone. Many people were gone in a short time—the doc's wife, the therapist, the bodyguard, and what about Grimes? Was there something more there?

He rounded the bend and headed up into the canyon toward the interstate, a good 27 miles away. There was no moon to offer any backlighting and if it wasn't for the stars, he might never have noticed the trees, tall pines, blocking out the sky. He checked his mirrors and caught the light behind him. A car's headlights, he presumed, and it reminded him to flick on his 'brights'.

Why would the senator want them to think that his son was a player when he must've known he was gay? It's not adding up.

He saw the lights of the trailing car now moving up fast. *This guy must be in a big hurry*, he thought. He made it around another blind curve and found a turnout where he pulled aside to let the racer go by to avoid any kind of unwanted encounter. He idled there, checking the mirrors, waiting, then wondering when the car never came. He waited a few moments more and then eased back onto the highway. *Strange...*

Steely blue eyes continued to monitor the mirror for a bit, and he returned to his thinking.

The man in black at the caution tape, Agent Wright? Could they be the same guy? And what's with all the cloak-and-dagger stuff, anyway, is a senator really that high profile?

He crested a small climb and caught the headlights again in the rearview. They were moving faster this time. He was not pulling over again. *If this is some kind of game, let's get to it,* he thought.

Maybe this was the follow-up to the bar attack. It would be a great place to take someone out. No witnesses, no cameras... the lights disappeared again.

The road dipped and he could make out the glow of a small town in the valley, way off in the distance. Somehow, it made him feel a little more comfortable—less alone or isolated.

What am I missing? The doc, the therapist, the bouncer, and now the new info on Corrina, all in the same place?

He turned a sharp winding stretch of road and, continuing his descent to the interstate, found himself almost completely blacked out by the trees. When he came out of the last turn, the headlights were there, pressing him. There were no turnouts in sight, no safe place to let him pass, so he slowed, hoping the car would go by on the oncoming traffic side. But the lights just pressed closer.

His eyes filled the mirror, and he felt a light tap on the bumper. The car broke loose for a second and the back end wiggled until the automatic rear wheel tracking engaged and brought it back under control. Barnes was furious and accelerated, trying to get some space between them.

He hit the brakes, hoping to force the driver to pass rather than crash, but the car slowed in time and still managed to apply the pressure. It infuriated Barnes at this point, and he became a bit frantic as he worked through the next tactic.

The road turned from straight into severe bends, alternating from left to right. Barnes had his eyes glued to the mirror again as he tried to pull away from the rushing vehicle. In fact, he spent more time in the rear and side-view mirrors at this point than on the road in front of him.

When he could finally straighten it out, something darted out across the road ahead of him.

He saw it in the headlights. It was just an instant, but he saw her. He saw her smile, that smile he missed so badly just seconds before he slammed into her and catapulted her into the air. His beloved Patricia...

"AAARRRGGGHHH!" He woke up screaming again, saturated in sweat, hands still gripping an imaginary steering wheel. He was furious and grabbed the digital clock. Heaving it at the wall, half of it shattered. It left the other half impaled in the sheetrock.

His pulse was racing, his anxiety was through the roof, and he paced nervously for 10 minutes before finally calming enough to get a drink of water to settle down.

I guess this'll never end. It's my fault. This is my price to pay.

CHAPTER 25

"You're busting my balls, right? Are you freaking kidding me?" The senator was stomping around the suite like an angry hippo. "Not only did we not send the right message, but they caught one of our messengers?"

Agent Wright remained stoic. "They won't talk. There's nothing that will find its way back to us."

"There darn well better not be! This entire situation is turning into a FUBAR state of affairs." The senator swilled down a double whisky on the rocks, resting a hand on his hip. "These were your best guys?"

"They've never failed us before, Senator." The agent stood strong.

"All we needed to do was send a message to an old cop who probably doesn't want this case anyway."

"I believe they received the message. We have tape that says he has just about had enough and wondered what he was even doing here in the first place." Wright stared forward. "That's almost a direct quote after leaving the bar that night."

"Good, we're still listening then?" The senator tugged at his suspenders.

"Yes, we also know that he's headed out to meet with Nichols tomorrow morning," the agent responded.

"What do they want with the doc? He should be cleared, just a witness to the crime, according to the detectives..."

"It seems they found some information on the doc's dead wife that ties her to the strip club bouncer. We picked that up earlier today when they went to lunch. They're heading up the mountain tomorrow." The agent twisted into a wry smile.

"Why wasn't I aware of this? I need that information... the information on the doc's wife, I mean. We have resources inside. We need to leverage them, and quickly," the senator fumed. "This is just another self-inflicted wound..."

"I'll make the calls."

"Mason has really messed this up. I told him to shut things down for a while, but it may be too far out of hand now." The senator continued pacing wildly across the room, huffing and puffing with every turn.

His bodyguard eyed him patiently. "I gave him your message directly, sir, but he said he had things under control."

"Do things appear under control to you?" The senator poured another whisky double. "I was counting on your persuasive abilities."

"You know Mason, sir. He wouldn't even listen to you. What makes you think he'd listen to me?" Agent Wright sighed.

"Even after all we did to clean up the mess he made in our own backyard," the senator rumbled. "He just never understood the big picture and that may have cost him his life."

The agent waited.

"We're going to have to make some very hard decisions. I've already experienced one irreplaceable casualty and I've got to protect the rest." The senator stopped his huffing and looked at Agent Wright. "We cannot allow this to go any further."

"I'm not sure things are that bad. There's nothing in our intel that tells us he's getting closer to resolving this…"

"Come now, you're smarter than that. Even this old codger of a detective will soon piece things together. If he's got something that ties the bouncer to the doc's wife, he's connecting dots and we know where that trail leads."

"This has been a very successful operation. We do not want to overreact," Agent wright argued. "His focus is splintered. He's still coping with the death of his wife."

"Yes, I heard about that and thought it might play in our favor. Yet, he seems to make steady progress. There's just far too much at stake here and the fallout could be catastrophic…" He paused. "For all of us. You understand?"

"Senator?" The agent smiled. "What would you like me to do?"

"I think we need to slow this train down and buy some time to mop up this branch."

"Yes, sir," the agent agreed. "What are the next steps?"

"We'll need to start by getting all of the players on the same page."

"Yes, sir, I'll make the necessary contacts," the agent volunteered. "Shall I have them assembled here?"

"No, neutral ground or they may get scared, and we need to get complete cooperation if we're going to pull this off."

"You have a time in mind?"

The senator was still thrashing the steps of his plan around. "No later than tomorrow night—non-negotiable. Everyone needs to be present."

"I'll see to it." The agent adjusted his suit. "Is that all?"

"No…no, it is not." The senator rubbed furiously at his eyes, trying to quell the building ache behind them.

"Senator…"

"We need to ensure that the case is slowed. We have one more crack at this. Send another message. A much more impactful message to the detective, and make it count. If you get my meaning?"

"I do, sir. Consider it done."

CHAPTER 26

"You really expect that letting him know we were on our way to visit was the right strategy?" Colt wrestled with the decision as the Crown Victoria came to a rolling stop next to a beautiful fountain that centered a turnabout driveway, fronting a six-car garage. "Shouldn't we have cold-called and caught him off guard?"

Barnes was quick to respond, "No, I thought about that, but I'd really prefer him to feel as though we're concerned about him and that this is a routine follow-up. I don't want him on high alert walking in."

Doc Nichols lived in an old, refurbished home on top of the bluff, overlooking the harbor in Rocky Point. On the outside, the dwelling appeared cold and foreboding. It was basically a castle that was moved over from Scotland, stone by stone, and reassembled by a wealthy family in 1902. Both detectives were in awe of the magnitude of the tremendous façade as they paused on the stone paved driveway.

"I clearly made the wrong career choice, kid," remarked the senior officer as he regarded the ostentatious home.

"You and me both. Sheesh, how much do you suppose something this big costs?"

"I don't even want to think about it. I feel small enough just standing in front of it."

Dressed in a smoking jacket over expensive silk pajamas, Doc Nichols responded to the knock on the oversized, 10-foot doors and plodded to the foyer to greet the detectives.

"Gentlemen, you needn't have made the long trip, but thank you both for coming out to check on me," Doc Nichols said after opening the door to his estate. "I suppose I could've come into town, but I haven't yet returned to work. That incident at the beach really took a lot out of me."

"Say no more," Barnes offered, extending a hand in greeting. "Witnessing something like that would weather anyone. Besides, I'm sure the rest is well-deserved. They must miss you at the hospital, though?"

"Oh, the hospital will do just fine without me. It's the clinic that concerns me," Doc replied, looking at his shaking hands. "Those people have nowhere else to go. But I'm afraid I'm just not ready to help in this condition."

"I'm sure it'll just take a little more time, Doc," Barnes reassured the doctor. "You'll be back to full speed before you know it."

The elder physician squeezed his hands into fists to arrest the quivering. "I wish I shared your optimism, Detective. I'm sorry, I haven't even invited you in and it's drizzling still. Please, gentlemen, come in, come in."

Once inside the home, the detectives realized the stark contradiction in style. The doctor completely remodeled the interior after purchasing it and had spared no expense in bringing it up to contemporary standards. Barnes regarded the estate as the epitome of luxury. Calacatta marble floors extended from the entryway into the home as far as they could see with fine inlaid designs that highlighted the almost entirely white interior with a brilliant black contrast.

High vaulted ceilings were home to dimmed track lighting and lavish crystal chandeliers. A long, winding spiral staircase rose to the second floor, just feet away from the entrance, framing a brightly lit hallway where mirrors hung over elaborately crafted metal and glass antique console tables and small couches. A tremendous sitting room opened to their right.

An enormous fireplace set entirely in polished stone was the featured item on the far wall, which bordered the outside. A grand piano sat in the corner adorned by pictures that ran along a large mantel and hung on the wall. The opposite side was home to French-style couches and chairs with carefully placed lights, which appeared to be for reading as a wall full of shelves held books of all subjects.

"Can I get you gentlemen something to drink?" Nichols queried considerately. "You must be thirsty after that drive?"

"Water would be fine." Barnes stepped into the sitting room, eyes drawn to another picture of Corrina on the piano.

Noble echoed the request and the doc disappeared briefly.

The detectives perused the room, both resting on the litany of photos. Pictures with the mayor, the councilman, and family were expected. Then there were those with famous people—a president or two, a big-name actor. Some hunting and other vacation photos trailed onto the mantel.

Nichols returned with two tall glasses of water. "I hope this is refreshing enough."

"I'm sure this'll be fine, thanks, Doc," Barnes returned. "You sure know a lot of high-profile people."

"Ah, yes, I've lived on the planet for quite a while now." He laughed. "I've been fortunate to meet a lot of important figures, most of whom have been a part of the charities and organizations that I work with and support. These are some very influential folks. Presidents, heads of state, foreign dignitaries, all invited here for fundraising events."

"All invited here, you say?" Barnes made eye contact.

"Yes, usually a semi-annual event, almost always on the new year and the 4th of July. It seems it's easier to rally the troops together when we can tie a great party with the cause."

"I imagine that's true. Still, it's a very impressive group of folks," Barnes recognized.

Nichols nodded and smiled.

"Colt here made me aware of the foundations you support, and I must admit, I'm in awe."

"Think nothing of it, Detective. I do what I can to help… well, like you are doing now."

"Yes, of course," Barnes answered, pulling out his notepad. "Speaking of which, I know that was quite a morning at the beach, and along with checking in on you, we wanted to circle back and see if anything else may have come to mind that might help us with this investigation?"

Nichols moved slowly to a small black couch and sat. He rested his head in his hands before running his fingers through his thin grey hair and stared forward into the floor. "I've done little but replay that event in my mind these past days and I confess that there is a small bit of confusion on my part. I was in a dead sleep when all heck broke loose. But I believe I have given you the most accurate accounting of events that I can. I'm sorry I cannot help you gentlemen more."

"I understand completely, Doctor. We certainly don't want to dredge up any more anxiety for you." Barnes tapped his pencil loudly and then, motioning to Noble, moved toward the front door. "I guess our work here is done, then. If there's anything we can do to help…"

"No, I'm sure I'll be fine with a bit more rest. I appreciate you checking in on me, but you do not need to feel responsible," the doc called over his shoulder. "If I recall any other information or if there is any other way I can help…"

Barnes turned sharply as the old physician stood to see them out. "Actually, there is something I'm curious about?"

"Of course, Detective, what is it?"

"Well, I hate to ask you this, given the strain of recent events. However, during our investigation, we came across some interesting information regarding your wife?"

The doctor turned two shades of pale and returned to his sitting position on the French sofa.

CHAPTER 27

The weight of the suggestion hung in the air like a vapor. Even Colton became uncomfortable in the deafening silence. The thick, voluminous clouds outside gathered together and fell on the house like a dark blanket. As they exploded and soaked the property with heavy droplets, drumming on the rooftop in rhythmic waves, the tired doctor regained his composure.

"Yes, Detective, what can I answer for you?" Nichols returned in a hushed voice without even looking in his direction.

"Well, our records indicate that she once worked at a strip club—Lovergirls, in fact. Were you aware of her background?"

"Are you making a judgement of some kind about the woman I married, the one person I love? At a time like this when two people have just lost their lives in our town?"

"No judgement whatsoever, Doc." Barnes remained calm. "We all have our pasts to contend with. What I was interested in is any connection she may have had with the two men we're investigating since one held a job as a bouncer at that same club. Documents indicate he once came to her aid in an unpleasant situation. You understand that this connection could place you on the suspect list?"

Nichols turned toward the detectives and the fatigue was visible in every line on his face. It appeared as if he was aging in front of them. "I cannot fathom the idea that you are this insensitive. My wife is dead. I'm still grieving, for crying out loud!"

The words sliced through Barnes like a razor. He squashed the memory of his own loss and continued. "I realize this is uncomfortable. We have a double homicide to resolve. These are questions, not accusations, Doctor. I know you understand. You have similar challenges in your line of work. I'm certain of that."

Noble moved inconspicuously across the room and fetched a glass of water from the tray, handing it to the old doc.

Nichols took a slow sip, nodding at the young detective as he did. His tired face turned angry. He had prepared for this eventuality. He spoke slowly and deliberately. "There is nothing that Corrina and I hid from one another. I'm aware of where she worked and of her past..." He paused at length to wrestle with his emotions.

"Doc," Barnes waited.

Nichols raised a hand as if requesting some time to gather himself. "She came by the clinic one night, late, after work... visibly shaken. She'd been in an altercation at the club and was crying in pain. Mascara ran down her cheeks and her arms cradled her stomach. Being the only physician on duty, I got to her just as she collapsed on the floor. The bleeding was profuse..."

Barnes thought it best to back off a bit. "Bleeding?"

"A gentleman had paid for a private room and a special session in her company a couple of months prior. He had forced himself on her when they were alone, took what he wanted like some savage animal." The doc took another sip of water and his shaking hands appeared almost uncontrollable. "She never disclosed it. She just didn't want any trouble."

Barnes could see Nichols growing more tired as he recounted the story. "Take your time, Doc."

"She informed him of the pregnancy and his answer was to punch her multiple times in the stomach. And he then tried to force her into a sexual act right in the middle of the club."

"He got what he deserved, that lowlife piece of—" Noble chimed in until Barnes quieted him with a wave.

"If one bouncer hadn't jumped into the fray, it might have been a lot worse. She lost the baby, of course, and the damage was extensive to her internally. The recovery process was long and costly."

"You cared for her the whole time, didn't you?" Barnes asked.

"Yes, Detective, she had no one to help her. No one to turn to for comfort, apart from a dysfunctional family of addicts." Tears glistened on the doc's cheeks.

"You paid all the bills and watched over her, nursed her back to health, and she fell in love with you? Is that right?" Barnes reasoned.

"I fell in love with her first. Her heart was amazing. Even after all that animal had done to her, she wouldn't press charges.

Instead, she forgave him and just wanted to move on." The doc cracked a crooked smile. "Her outer charm was incredible, but her inner beauty was even more compelling. I had no chance against it. I would've done just about anything for her, so I married her and took her away from all the ugliness to what I hoped was a better life."

"But she was never able to escape?" Barnes asked.

Colton had set the tablet on record and kept looking at it to make sure it was working.

"Oh, things were great for a while. We had those trips to the beach that I told you about. She seemed so happy, like all her worries were in the past. But you can never outrun yourself."

"What do you mean?" Noble asked.

"I mean, she couldn't get away from her pain. The hurt of the lost baby, of the family issues. I don't know, but she became addicted to prescription meds. It soon became the only time she was ever happy…when she was high, that is."

"So, why did you avoid telling us about this before if you knew?"

"I didn't know the dead men, Detective. And quite frankly, this is between my wife and me. There's no need to further sully her memory."

"I'm so sorry for bringing this to your doorstep again, Doc." Barnes' sincerity was not in question. "I'm trying to find answers…"

"It's more than that, Detectives." The doc broke down, and like the breaking of a dam, the water poured out.

The two detectives looked at each other.

"Where do you think she got the meds…?"

CHAPTER 28

Her breathing was heavy, the walls felt like they were closing in on her. The further she ran, the more she realized there just wasn't enough space to get lost or hide. She finally made her way past the commercial buildings and instantly felt relieved when her feet hit the sand and the pain of the rough street subsided. But there was no time to rest. She had to put as much distance between her and those men as she could before they realized she was gone. So, she continued to dash ahead toward the light she had used to set her course.

Fortunately for her, the evening mist made the sand wet, so it was a bit easier to move on. For that, she was thankful, but the hanging moisture was just heavy enough to make her wet and the cold was piercing through her dampened clothes. After a while, she realized the light she had seen was coming from a lighthouse in the distance. She wondered where she was… there were no lighthouses left in L.A.

She needed to get out of the rain and find a place to dry off and rest. The lighthouse appeared as safe as anywhere at this point, so she set her sights on the huge beacon and made her way there as quickly as her legs would carry her, keeping to the edge of the fence and along the tree line.

It was only minutes later that she heard the squeal of tires as the fake ambulance sped through the commercial district, searching frantically for the missing body. It zoomed down streets and alleys in a crisscross pattern, ensuring every trash bin and dark corner had been checked. He figured she couldn't have gone too far.

When he struck out amongst the buildings, the vehicle pulled to a stop at the edge of the beach and, after a few seconds, a huge and powerful beam began to sweep over the sand dunes, trying to search her out.

She hit the ground behind a large tree and didn't move. The light continued to sweep over the beach and the gruff-voiced man was moving toward her. He made it about halfway and scanned the tree line to the edge where the cliffs were, and then screamed out loud.

"You stupid bitch, you would've at least been alive. Now I will find you and kill you if you do not come back. It's your only chance. Don't be stupid. I will hunt you down."

His partner had secured the building and found his way to where the van was. He called to his buddy, "Come on, there's just not enough time, you'll never find her. We need to relocate before it's too late."

"This stupid girl has ruined everything! AARRGGHH!" he yelled and trudged through the sand back to the van. But before he piled in, he thought he would be crafty and took one more sweep of the dunes behind him, hoping she had moved.

She was smart and remained hidden until the van had left and the area was clear for at least 15 minutes. Pulling a couple of large palm fronds over her, she dodged most of the wetness. An hour later, she noticed the white van speed away from the site.

They had returned and loaded the other girls back into the van, cleaned the rooms, and wiped the place free of any fingerprints or possible DNA evidence.

She wasn't taking any chances though and waited another 10 minutes just in case they were trying to trick her into a false sense of security, and then the flashlight came again. It scanned the buildings, the streets, and then the beach area one more time after the ambulance passed by, hoping to flush her out.

"I told you, you won't find her. We're wasting time, and I don't want to go back to prison." She caught the driver talking. "Come on, let's go."

"You know they'll kill us if we don't find her?" the shorter gruff man argued.

"They may kill you, but I'm dropping these other three girls off back at the central site and you'll never hear from or see me again...I'm gone like the wind, brother."

"They'll catch you." The gruff voice filled the night air. "We have to find this girl."

"If we leave the bodies in the transfer building and this girl makes it to the cops, we go to jail or get killed, or both. If we take these girls back and report the girl missing, we get killed. The longer we're around here, the more dead we are."

The gruff talker was freaking out. "We're hosed, man. We're freaking hosed."

"Are you coming, or do you want me to leave you here to be wasted by Rafa's goons?"

"Okay, okay, but when we get there, we call 'Gridlock'. If he says we're cool, everything should be alright." His scratchy voice was getting shaky.

"Are you an idiot? We definitely call to give them the best chance at covering down, but I'm out. I'm hitting the road like a bullet train. I ain't waiting for somebody to come and kill me. They are going to have to chase my ass all over the map if they want to find me."

"We're leaving a lot of money on the table here, bro. I need that money." The gruff guy was not thinking straight.

"Get in the freaking car now or I'm leaving your ass behind. We gotta get moving fast to have any chance of survival, bro. I shut down the internal security cams, but they're going to be checking and probably soon. We're out of time. We can't look for this girl and stay alive, so pick one. This vehicle leaves in 5, 4, 3…"

The other guy reluctantly piled into the van and it took off. She watched and waited, then waited some more. It was getting warm under the palm fronds and she fell asleep…quiet, warm, fuzzy but not induced. Exhausted but safe.

CHAPTER 29

"Sheesh, Brad. What the heck was that?" Noble talked under his breath after stepping out of Doc's place. The wind had turned fierce and whipped at the long flaps of his trench coat. "I haven't seen that side of you before."

With the last downpour, the temperature had dropped, and Barnes hustled, anxious to get back to the car. "I needed his reaction to be raw. That's why I timed it that way. I waited until we were on the way out and his defenses were down before asking about Corrina."

"You came on kind of strong, don't you think? I thought we were going to lose him and he was going to shut down on us." Noble swung the door open and jumped into the Crown Vic, avoiding a puddle.

"It was a possibility, but I didn't accuse and I never lacked compassion. It was just designed to get the answers we need without dancing around the issue. I wanted to get to the point, quickly." Barnes felt a cold shiver run through him and his mind drifted back to the accident on the coast highway. *Get to the point*; it triggered him. Patricia had said it. Was she guiding him, even then? He thought on that for just a minute before slipping the key in the ignition and starting the car.

"Well, I could've used a heads-up. It got uncomfortable…"

"It had to be real. Everyone's reactions needed to be real, even yours."

"Are you testing me, too? Am I missing something here, partner?"

"No, Colt, but people can pick up on things, reactions, movements…"

Noble shook his head and some moisture sprayed on Barnes. "This must be more of that L.A. Detective 101 shit you learned back there?"

"Thanks for the shower, kid." The senior detective shot his cohort a terse look. "No, there's very little substitute for experience, kid. I learn something new every day."

"Me too. I learned you have two sides, and one of them isn't so nice."

"We've all got that in us, Colt." Barnes laughed. "But I just learned another lesson in patience. While we were sitting here gabbing like two schoolgirls, I saw Nichols pull the drapes back and check on us to see if we left." He backed away from the fountain and edged the car forward.

"So, is that some big thing I should understand?" Noble asked. "Do you believe his story?"

"Maybe, maybe not, but it just doesn't feel right to me. None of this feels right. I'm missing something important."

Barnes turned the car out onto the two-lane road leading back down the hill to town. He thought he heard Patricia whisper again. *Listen and you will hear.*

"You know, we've still got that warrant for the therapist's office we haven't moved on yet..." Noble observed.

"Yeah, and I want to do some research on the senator, see if I can learn a bit more about him." Barnes scratched at his stubble as they continued along the flat rim of the highway.

"Wait...now you think the senator plotted to kill his own kid?" Noble looked confused. "You can't possibly be serious. Are you making him a suspect?"

"I'm looking at everything and everyone at this point. I'm not sure where I'm at with the doc and his story or the senator, but if I can link the two of them..." Barnes could just make out the harbor below. He was in his own head now, searching, asking, and wondering...trying to put things together. *Slow down*, he thought he heard Patricia's voice again.

"Well, it occurs to me that the doc was genuinely distraught over the loss of his wife. Maybe even guilty because of the meds," Noble commented. "Is there a prosecution trail there? I mean, that's a confession, right? I have him on the recording..."

"If you were listening, he admitted nothing. Any defense lawyer worth his weight would get it thrown out. What he said was, 'Where do you think she got the meds...?'

"But you and I know that's what he meant. We were there."

"That doesn't matter, Colt. It's what he said, not what he implied." Barnes sighed. "I've been involved in enough lost cases and courtrooms to know that. I imagine the doc has faced a lot of litigation as well. Maybe that's why he was so careful."

A big rig with a flatbed full of logs whisked by with only inches between them and threw a trail of mist in their direction. Barnes hit the wipers to clear his view and navigated a switchback of quick turns cut into the mountainside as the road dropped on its way into the valley.

"More L.A. Detective 101 stuff."

"Will you knock that off and just listen?" Barnes was trying to think.

With each new corner, he noticed something strange. The brakes were getting spongy and he had to push harder to get them to engage. Then, all at once, his foot was on the floorboard and they weren't working at all.

The car was picking up speed when it should have been slowing. "Brad, we're not in a race here. We're going downhill."

The winding road limited visibility. Rain and the occasional oncoming car made it difficult to keep the Crown under control.

"I know that!" he barked. "Oh, crap…we've got a big problem." Barnes was stomping on the pedal. "We've lost the brakes, kid. This isn't going to end well."

Colt looked over his shoulder. "Nobody behind us. You can pitch it and maybe we get a break."

"Not in these corners. We could take out another car, maybe women and children. Not going to do that."

Barnes tried engine braking and downshifted into second gear, hoping to reduce speed. The car lurched and fought back, the engine over revved and they slowed a little, but with the twisting lanes, it was still too dangerous to try and pitch it sideways.

"Colt, you can bail out if you want, might be your best chance." Barnes fought the car through another swerving set of esses.

"Nah, I'd probably break every bone in my body. I'll take my chances."

Barnes tried downshifting again and, this time, the change was too much to take. The car jerked wildly. The transmission gears splintered, the driveshaft locked and froze the rear tires, and the car went into a power slide.

Out of habit, Barnes pressed on the brake pedal that wouldn't respond. There was a loud pop and black smoke billowed out of the hood.

Colt had both legs completely extended and wedged himself against the seat with his arms pressed against the roof. "Ohhh, crap." Colt could see a large pickup truck coming up the hill in the oncoming lane.

The Crown Vic was now hydroplaning on the wet asphalt, drifting slowly into the other lane. Barnes flashed back to the accident that took his wife. He still blamed himself and now he was at the wheel with his partner's life on the line. It was a lot to digest.

"Brad…"

"I see it, kid." Barnes spun the wheel quickly to the right and then immediately back to the left, just managing to miss the oncoming pickup truck. He then turned into the spin and the car skidded with the back end coming around. They slid off the shoulder and down a slight embankment until impacting some enormous pine trees. It punctuated the stop with a loud boom. Windows exploded, sending glass in all directions, and the airbags were deployed. The knocking engine had seized, and the two detectives sat in silence momentarily.

Colt checked himself for injuries. His neck ached and his back was tight, but other than that, he was okay. "You alright, Brad?"

"Yeah, I'm just freaking fine."

"This was one accident I wasn't sure I was walking away from." Colt brushed away some shattered glass and tried to open his door.

"Something tells me this was not an accident." Barnes was still sitting, hands glued to the steering wheel with a vice-like grip when his phone chimed.

"You think it's another message?" Colt managed to wedge the door open.

Barnes raised a hand in the air to quiet Colt and fumbled around, trying to connect the ring to the phone's location. It had fallen on the floorboard in front of his seat. He twisted his stiff frame and retrieved it. "This is Detective Barnes…"

Colton looked at him as if he was crazy for taking the call in that moment.

"Thanks for taking the time to call, Kayleigh...no, I don't think you need to leave. But just in case, I'll send a black and white over to watch things. We'll be there as soon as we can."

She thanked him and hung up.

"Nope, this was more than a message. I'd say this was an attempt to take us out. That was the therapist's assistant. She said two big goons came by and rummaged through the office. Somebody does not want us finding answers. I thought we might've stumbled into a hornet's nest, but now I'm certain."

CHAPTER 30

It took a couple of hours before the tow truck arrived, but it was still light when the detectives stepped out of the huge diesel flatbed that idled so loud in front of the station.

"Colt, can you work on getting us another vehicle? I want to get over to Kayleigh today. In the meantime, I'm going to do a brief internet search on the senator while the official background report is being generated." They were past the busy front office and the desk sergeant buzzed them in without so much as a nod.

"You're not still thinking he killed his own kid?"

"No, I'm thinking there's more to him than meets the eye. I could be wrong, but it's worth the investment of time."

"Got it. Let me try and finagle us a new ride." Colton rubbed at his sore neck and headed down the hallway.

Barnes grabbed a quick cup of coffee, jammed a toothpick between gritting teeth, and dropped into the swivel chair at his desk. *Alright, Senator William Walker, let's see who you are.* He opened his browser and typed in the name, then hit the return key. Multiple images littered the screen of the senator, but they didn't all resemble the man Barnes had met.

He recalled Agent Wright's elevator description, 'second-term, second-generation' and understood. This must be his father. He perused the files and read quickly, assimilating any valuable information.

Barnes thought back on the pompous Walker Jr. and realized, *It's no wonder these guys are full of themselves.* The pictures he perused showed the senior senator getting out of limousines or attending gala events dressed in tuxedos, smiling, standing next to other politicians or actors, models, and even presidents. It was a vanity fest, to be certain. Then it hit him…

This was a familiar face. He'd seen this guy before, seen pictures of him. It took only seconds, but he was sure he'd seen this guy in the pictures at old Doc Nichols' place. Sure, younger versions of both men, but he was positive it was them.

This was just too much of a coincidence. His mind raced and he clicked on picture after picture, trying to talk himself out of the likeness being the elder senator. But no matter the number of photo references, he only became surer—this was the guy in those pictures. *There's got to be a bigger connection here. Did the doc have something on the Walkers? Did the Walkers have something on the old doctor? Were they simply friends? If so, how did they know each other?*

He wasn't finding a quick connection but knew he had to dig deeper. He really wanted the official report on Walker Jr., but with a quick email, he now extended the report to the father and Doc Nichols.

While he waited, he decided to look for individual pages or articles, other informational sites, business pages, etc. There had to be a link, and he needed to find it.

Nothing came up on Facespace or Quikipedia on the senior Walker except that he was a U.S. senator. For Walker Jr. and Doc Nichols, it was the typical bio stuff, birthdates, some family history, and educational information. But there weren't any clear links that put them together. They came from different walks of life—a politician and a physician.

Colt returned with a set of keys to find Barnes focused on his screen. "Ready to roll when you are."

"Gimme a minute," Barnes was short with his tone.

Colt fell in behind, looking over his shoulder. "You found something?"

"Well, maybe. I was looking at the senator and found his father's references as well. I would never have known it had we not gone to visit the doc, but this guy was in a couple of the photos on the mantel."

"You're not kidding?" He almost gushed.

"There's a link between these guys, I'm sure of it. I've just got to keep looking and I'll find it." Barnes continued searching page after page but was unable to solve the puzzle and knew he had to get out to talk with Kayleigh before it got too late.

Before leaving, he sent a desperate email to the address at the Connecticut library that had tipped him off on the senator's son's court debacle back in his hometown years earlier.

He asked for any known connections between the Walkers and Nichols. Addressed to User@Connpublib.com, it was a long shot, he was aware, but he figured a loose ball in the right hands could change the outcome of a game.

I wonder if Fairbanks could help. Maybe it's time to make that call?

CHAPTER 31

After the last of those in attendance found their seats, Agent Wright took up a position sitting behind the senator, who nursed a scotch whisky double, dry. Around the small table, a few key players gathered for the meeting.

Donned in a lengthy red dinner dress with slits up the sides, Sable, the club owner of Lovergirls, nervously smoked one of her long, thin cigarettes. She brought her security man, 'G', to look out for her. He scanned the room to get familiar with the ingress and egress points, then vetted the potential threats, settling on the agent and two Latino men before taking his seat.

Rafa, who ran the facility where the 'assets' were housed before distribution, was there with his partner, Miguel. Both were enormous, muscled men with tattoos that covered all of their bodies, including their necks and shaved heads. None of the players in attendance had ever met the others or even knew of them. Plausible deniability was of prime importance in case any trouble came.

The Mayor of Rocky Point was the last to arrive. Of the entire group, his level of nervousness was the most obvious.

Empty chairs at the end of the table caught his eye but he was the only one to ask, "Are we expecting more?"

Senator Walker Jr. set his drink on the table and sent a burning stare into the mayor's face but didn't speak.

The tension was monumental. Mayor Moyer looked from person to person to find only blank expressions. "It's a logical question. There are three empty seats."

The senator's flat voice was penetrating, "Those seats are for members of our group who are no longer with us and should be a stark reminder of what happens to those of us who are uncommitted to the business or operate outside of the business."

They all looked at each other.

"Now, I need to know what has happened here," the senator barked. "Anyone?"

No one responded.

"You all realize what is at stake here, right? We're talking millions of dollars, and that's if we only shut this operation down temporarily." Winslow was direct. "I've put something in motion to buy us time but have to decide quickly, tonight, and I'd prefer it to be based on factual information and potential consequences."

The mayor drummed his fingers. Rafa and Miguel stared straight forward, and Sable shifted closer to her security man.

"Now, I pay you all a tremendous amount of money to keep this running smoothly. Tell me we are clean. I have to know what we're facing here. We have made far too many mistakes. Lives have been lost. Sable, the cops have an eyewitness who

I trust. They tell me a bodyguard who once worked for you killed my son. He would've filled empty seat number one. But he's no longer here. I just identified his body and made arrangements to get his remains shipped back to Connecticut for a funeral.

The Lovergirls manager was slow to respond.

"I'm waiting." His scowl was penetrating. "You see, a lot of assets end up in your club. You make money off of them after they have been broken. We can't have the cops sniffing up our tree. We pay inside money to avoid pressure from the police."

"Yes, sir," Sable acknowledged.

"Well, are we compromised?" he yelled and slammed a fist on the table, spilling his drink.

'G' stood up to reach into his jacket but stopped when he heard the sound of a shotgun cocking behind the senator.

"Now that we have your attention." He smiled coldly at 'G' until he returned to his seat. "Can you answer the question please, Sable?"

"The cops came by and asked a lot of questions, but it'll take them forever to figure this out. They don't even know who Mason Walker is."

The senator laughed. "So, you think that the 25-year LAPD missing persons detective is backwoods? He met with us a couple of days ago, he knows exactly who Mason is."

"He was LAPD? He didn't seem to have a clue." She looked at 'G.'

"He's been out of the game a while, but once he gets the scent, we could be in trouble. That's why we're here. I need to know what you all know."

"Oh, crap," Sable muffled.

"Why was your bodyguard on the beach with my son?"

"I don't know," she stammered. "He quit more than a month ago. Said he had places to go and things to do. Percy Sutherland was a good guy."

"Did you say Sutherland?" Rafa asked. "Big African-American guy?"

"Yes, that's him," Sable answered, looking around the room, confused.

"Mason was going to bring him into the organization." Rafa motioned to the senator.

"We don't just 'bring someone into the organization,'" Walker fumed.

"Precisely why we never let him meet any of the players or visit any facilities," Miguel reinforced. "We know protocol."

"This is amazing. You have to be kidding me?" The senator shifted in his chair. "Rafa, we had a near miss a few months ago with that young girl. What was her name?"

"Reagan."

"Yes, Reagan. We nearly lost an asset that could have turned us a lot of money and we've had to sit on that, waiting for the right time to move. We had to give up the property, pay a lot of money to find the two responsible for that near catastrophe, and dispose of them. Now you're telling me we invited an unknown into the mix. Are there any links to us?"

"No, sir, we shut that down. The first mistake with the girl was a freak accident, according to our inside intel. Grimes told us why that happened and cleaned up the mess." Rafa was confident. "We did not slip up again."

"Ah, yes, seat number two. One of our inside men, Ben Grimes, the former lead detective here in Rocky Point. A case of a change of heart that needed a change of heart, so to speak." The senator pointed.

"Wait, you did Grimes? I thought he had a heart attack?" The mayor's face turned pale.

"You knew what you were getting into, Mr. Mayor. No one is out of our reach," Walker ranted. "I've never once heard you complain when the money funneled into your offshore accounts."

"But why Grimes? He cleaned up that mishap for us!" the mayor questioned.

"Ben was okay as long as he had no contact with any of the assets. When he took care of the mess that our transfer team fouled up, his hands got dirty meeting the girl. He contacted me and wanted out. Suddenly, he grew a conscience. Said if we didn't let him out, he was going to expose us. So, we gave him the only way out...some medicine to induce cardiac arrest. You understand now, I assume, Mr. Mayor?"

The mayor pushed away from the table and vomited on the floor between his legs. He had no color left in his face. Agent Wright laughed and tossed him a bottle of water.

"Things are just too messy. I think it's best to shut things down here for a while. We're going to need to reassemble a team that won't make mistakes," the senator concluded. "Just to be on the safe side."

"But we need that money and the assets in our club," Sable argued.

"Do you need that bad enough to go to prison?" the senator asked. "You can keep the club open. Closing it would only bring unwanted additional attention. It would paint a giant bullseye on the place. Ship out any local talent within the ring. You can work directly with Rafa and Miguel. Do not accept any recycled local talent. Once you've made those arrangements, take a vacation until things calm down. You can't be questioned that way."

"Yes, sir."

"Rafa, I'm going to play a hunch. Move everything and everyone we have in play. Wait two weeks and open a new facility. Check with me and we'll determine the next steps."

"Okay, Jefe," Rafa responded. "It is done."

"But you clean that facility like it was a bleach factory. No one can stumble in there and find anything that links it to our business. Am I reaching you?"

"It will be as you say."

"Mr. Mayor, I suggest you pull yourself together and start laying down the most sophisticated smokescreen you can dream of. I suspect attention will be diverted temporarily after our latest action to get these detectives off the trail. Do anything you can to slow this investigation without appearing obvious. Hold press conferences, meetings, ask questions, make executive decisions, and act like a mayor. You don't want to find yourself owning one of those empty seats." He flashed a Grinch-like grin. "Do you?"

"Of course not." He coughed. "By the way, who was seat number three?"

"More to come, Mr. Mayor." The senator looked at Agent Wright. "More to come."

CHAPTER 32

The sun dropped fast over the horizon, and the moon fought for visibility obscured by a canopy of dark clouds. An electrical storm was building, and the occasional lightning bolt flashed, burning the night sky above a light patter of misty drizzle.

After finding another vehicle—a far more 'experienced' mid-sized Ford—they arrived at the Canyon Drive office to meet with Kayleigh.

When they pulled in, they relieved the black and white for a dinner break and slotted into the parking space directly in front of the building. It was quite clear that Kayleigh was overanxious when the door opened well before they got close. She stood there with a cigarette in her mouth, nervously tapping her feet.

Barnes paused in front of her, lingering long enough to taste the sweet smell of tobacco as it danced in the air. After the near-deadly accident, he had been fighting off the strongest desire to light up since coming to Rocky Point.

"I guess this settles the question of your overactive imagination," Barnes offered some levity.

"What's going on?" Kayleigh blurted out after closing the door behind them. "Am I in danger? Why are these guys barging in here?"

"Did they accost you in any way? Are you hurt?" Noble asked.

"No, they were as disrespectful as could be, but nothing physical," she answered.

"Miss Crawford, Kayleigh," the older detective spoke in a subdued voice, hoping to drive her anxiety down. "I'm sure this was very frightening for you. Especially with everything that's going on. Let's all sit down and you can tell us what happened."

She took two more intense drags of her cigarette and smoke plumed in front of her. Kayleigh's frustration was visible, but it was the aroma from the fumes that distracted Barnes. His craving was peaking and he almost reached into his pocket to retrieve the emergency cigarette he'd replaced after the bar fight. *Just one cigarette. It can't be that bad.*

He doused the desire and reluctantly followed her as she led them to the waiting area. Miss Crawford paused until they sat, then took her position on folded legs in the same chair where she rested during the first visit.

Barnes removed his notepad and Colton reminded her he would record the conversation with her consent. She agreed and breathed into her fist as if to ready herself.

"Well, it was just after 2 pm when these guys came to the door. They knocked loudly and repeatedly like they were in a big hurry. So, I went to the door and opened it. Before I could even say anything, they were pushing their way in..."

"You said there were two of them, is that correct?" Barnes questioned.

"No, there were two goons...the big, slow, dumb type, and one sort of nerdy guy." She continued, "The big guys just started going through the desks in the office and out here. If they thought they found something, they brought it to the nerdy guy. I guess he was the brains of the group."

"Did they take anything?" Noble looked around the room. The goons had clearly ransacked the place. They left drawers open; papers and books lay scattered across the floor.

"Well, I'm sure I didn't see everything, but I know they took the appointment book. Oh, and they made off with Mason's laptop." She pointed toward the therapist's desk in the office behind her. "Then they asked me where his room was and headed up the stairs."

"Did you follow them?" Noble questioned.

"No, the nerdy guy told me to stay put, so I did." She shivered for effect. "I didn't want to be around them, anyway. I was thinking about running out, but before I did, they came back down."

Barnes flipped the pages on his notepad. "Did they say anything or ask questions about Mason?"

"No, they walked straight to the door and left. They didn't even look at me."

"So, you don't know if they took anything else?" Noble rubbed his aching neck again—the remnants of the accident after the interview with Nichols.

"I'd like a look around that space just the same, if you don't mind?" Barnes smiled at her and rose from the couch.

Kayleigh understood and led them up the stairs toward the senator's son's room. The conversation continued.

"There wasn't much in there for them to take. He had a bed, a dresser, a television, and a closet full of clothes. Unless they were into cosplay or something," she snickered.

"Cosplay?" Barnes appeared confused.

"It's a big thing these days, Brad. People dress up in costumes and role-play, like knights at the renaissance fair or Star Wars gatherings." Colton cleared the murky air. "It's a fairly large community."

Kayleigh added, "Mason used to leave here in costume and tell me he was going to conventions or parties. It got to be pretty regular. Sometimes he'd be gone the whole weekend."

Barnes reached the top of the stairs. "So, Halloween 365?"

"I guess it's kinda like that," Kayleigh answered. "When you say it that way, it does sound a bit weird, right?"

"I'm finding a lot of things weird in this case," Barnes said. "I guess you never know what people are into, what they're thinking..."

They arrived at the door to Mason's room and Noble pushed it open, peering inside. "I said it before, Brad. The world keeps turning and you can't stop it. You can only get off if it gets too much for you."

"That's a fact, Detective," Kayleigh remarked. "That simple conundrum filled a lot of therapy time for Mason. There are a lot of unhappy, unfulfilled people."

"Well, I suppose this dress-up was a release for the senator's kid?" But inside, Barnes was grinding gears, his mind was parsing data. Everything from the doc's wife, Corrina, to Grimes to Colton's lighthouse 'jumpers'. All getting off the spinning world.

"What a mess," Kayleigh sighed, stepping into the room.

"Careful what you touch, kid." Barnes put some rubber gloves on and tossed a pair to his partner.

Colton caught them and took a preliminary scan of the area. The drawers were all open and askew with clothes hanging over or on the floor. The bed was ruffled, and the top mattress looked as if someone had checked under it, hoping to find something hidden and important. In the closet were some suitcases and travel bags. The shelf above the hanging rack had been cleared and all the contents were strewn around the floor below. On the right side, the hangers all held costumes, everything from comic characters to Star Wars and Star Trek clothes, and then the simpler Harry Potter-type stuff, and police or firemen outfits.

Colton scanned the room with his tablet, videotaping and snapping some close-up photos.

Barnes noticed the dust on the dresser, which outlined where a ledger may have rested. "Does anything stand out to you that might be missing?"

"I couldn't be sure; I just don't know what was in here other than what I've already mentioned." Kayleigh lowered her head.

The detectives poked around in the room for about 20 more minutes before returning downstairs to the waiting area.

"We apologize for taking so much of your time, Kayleigh." Barnes placed a new toothpick in his teeth. "I'm sure it's been a long day for you and for us too. I think we're almost done."

"It was a bit scary, but I don't think they really cared about me." She smirked. "They just wanted Mason's stuff."

"You said you couldn't be sure what was missing from his room, but did it look like they had anything in hand when they left?" Barnes straightened his coat.

"They had a big binder or something that I could see and some things that were all balled up in a blanket, sort of like a knapsack that they carried."

Barnes removed the warrant from the inside of his coat and motioned to hand it to the assistant. "So, we know they took the appointment book from his office and a binder from his room. Shame, we were hoping to get a look at that calendar or appointment book..."

Kayleigh snickered. "Oh, you don't need that. What's the point now? They've already been through everything."

Barnes dropped the folded paper on the coffee table. "Yeah, I guess you're right. Still, losing that appointment book stings. I really hoped to get a look at the names on his patient list."

"That's not a problem. All of that stuff is online."

"Why the appointment books then?" Barnes appeared stymied. "If you kept all the records online?"

Kayleigh smiled. "We still needed signatures. It's legal, authorization for insurance payments, proof of visits, etc."

"But they took the computer, you said?" Barnes observed.

"They took Mason's computer, not mine. I sometimes keep mine with me at night to do bookkeeping. In this case, it was to keep in touch with family after the incident, you know, Facespace and email..."

"Did the goons go into your room?" Barnes asked.

"I don't know. I've been so anxious that I hadn't even thought to check." Kayleigh bolted from the chair and raced upstairs, returning a minute later with her laptop in hand.

Noble smiled as if he had just gone 'all-in' in a poker match against a bluffing opponent.

"Can you get into the database? Or would they have destroyed it by now?" Barnes asked.

"Sure." She opened the lid, flipped it on, and logged into the site they used for billing and records. "They would've needed his password or a very good hacker to get in."

Barnes watched over her shoulder while Noble checked his messages.

"Here we go," she said. "You can look at every appointment since we opened the place." She moved aside and allowed the detective to scroll through the list. It was cumbersome and slow, and he would need to write all the names. There were too many to recall.

"Is there a quicker way to get a list of patients?" He looked back at her.

"I never had the need, but yeah, let me in there a minute." She slid the detective to the side and took the keyboard.

Barnes watched in fascination as she exported the data into an Excel pivot table and then sorted it alphabetically.

"Here, you can scroll much quicker this way." She turned the screen toward the detective. "If you need more info, we can add sorting queries such as new or old patients, how many appointments they had, etc.

Noble moved closer now and they gave him a quick look through the list. "Let's start with the new patients," Barnes suggested.

Kayleigh adjusted the filters, and the most recent patients filled the table.

A quick look didn't raise any interest from either detective. "Okay, maybe it would be better the other way. Can you just reset it to the full list again, please?" Barnes asked.

She clicked a couple of boxes and things returned to their initial sorting state. "I'm going to get some water. Are either of you thirsty?" she offered.

"Bottled, if you have it?" Colton replied, moving into the spot she vacated next to Barnes.

"Me too, if you don't mind," Barnes added. He scrolled the mouse wheel down a couple of screens and the two of them looked through the names, neither making a sound. Two more-page jumps when it literally leaped off the screen and almost choked them by the throat.

Corrina Nichols.

CHAPTER 33

B arnes was still asleep when the phone rang. He reached for the nightstand and put the cellular to his ear.

"Hello, this is Detective Barnes," his groggy voice filled the room.

"I sure hope so because that's who I was calling," the councilman laughed.

"Jim, I'm sorry. I can't see too well when I first wake up. But it's great to hear that calming baritone voice of yours," Barnes chuckled.

"Well, don't feel too bad. I can't see too well no matter what the time of day," the councilman howled. "Listen, I'm headed your way. Can we meet for some breakfast? I think we need to talk."

Barnes did a mental check of what he had planned for the day. "Sure, Jim. Can you give me a half?"

"Of course. The diner in 30?"

The low rumble of thunder in the distance echoed in the morning's arrival and Barnes thought briefly about pulling the blankets over his head and catching some more z's.

"See you there." He clicked off and reluctantly hit the shower.

Thirty minutes later, he pulled into the parking lot of Rose's Diner on the northern bluff, just off of Highway 101, a quarter of a mile before the entrance to the beach parking lot. It was the first time the detective had been this close to the scene of the homicide since that day.

He paused for a couple of seconds, looking out over the beach and toward the lighthouse. He shook off the heebie-jeebies, wondering about Colton's 'jumpers' and how anyone could make a choice like that.

Clouds filled the landscape as far as he could see, and the thunder still hammered at the dark sky. He wondered when the storm might relent and stepped into the diner through the glass double doors just as the rain started to fall behind him.

"Great timing," the hostess chided. "Just one?"

"No, I'm meeting a friend," he told her.

"Oh, you must be here to see the councilman. He's in the back." The young girl smiled, and framed by her bright red hair, the space between her front teeth showed. "He told me to look out for you."

"Thanks." The detective headed toward the rear of the diner where the councilman held his hand in the air like a golf flag, marking the hole in a green. "Brad, it's good to see you."

"You too." He smiled. "What's up? You said we need to talk."

"Right to it, huh, bud?" Jim watched as his friend slid into the booth seat opposite him.

"I've got a case to solve, and I'm finally making some headway. If I can connect a couple of more dots…"

"Why didn't you tell me about the accident? And then I hear there was a fight or ambush of some sort at the Nest?" The councilman winced. "Are you okay?"

"I'm fine, Jim. The attack at the Crow's Nest didn't amount to much. And I'm not sure what caused the brakes to fail yet... the car is being looked at now so the jury is still out. But my gut tells me we're getting close to something big. I think they were just trying to warn us off."

"I'm getting worried about you, buddy. That's potentially two attempts on your life." Meyer paused. He shoveled in a fork full of undercooked hash browns. "We already lost Patricia. Can't afford to lose you as well."

"I'm fine, a little bruised...mostly my ego, but I'm fine." Barnes placed the menu like a screen between them to create some space.

"Okay, perhaps I'm overly concerned, but maybe we should call for help?"

"The feds?" Barnes plopped the menu on the table and leaned back into his seat. "They're not exactly on my 'favorite people to work with' list right now. You know, they had to buy off on deporting the driver who hit us. He should've received the death penalty or multiple life sentences at the least. All that pompous Fairbanks could tell me was their hands were tied."

"You and I can agree on that until the cows come home, but it won't mean anything if you're dead." The councilman laid his fork on the table with a clang. "They tried to get you twice, Brad. Twice."

"Nothing's confirmed on the car yet, and I've got a case to work on that you asked for my help with." Barnes eased up a bit before standing. "So, unless you're firing me..."

"No, come on now, relax. I just want to make sure you're okay. We've been friends for a long time and I feel responsible here. Because of that, if there's anything else that happens that places you in a similar situation, I'm making that call. Understood?"

"If the accident was an attempt, they can't try again. It's too obvious at this point. I'm getting close and I fear they'll pull away before I get closer, so I've got to work fast." He dropped a 20-dollar bill on the table. "Thanks for the coffee. Give that to the redhead."

The councilman picked up the 20 and handed it back to Barnes. "I can cover the tip, bud."

"Give it to her, Jim. She doesn't even know it but she's been a great help."

Meyer rose and shook hands, looking directly into his friend's tired eyes. "Please wrap this up, Brad. You're the best I know. But more importantly, be safe."

"Gimme some time. If you call in the feds, you'll be sounding the alarm. They'll abandon ship. We'll miss the opportunity to get the entire picture and bring these dirtbags to justice. It'll just string the case out longer and you don't want that." I've got some contacts within the bureau, let me make some calls." He excused himself.

Barnes stood at the entrance of the diner looking out at the beating rain. He pulled out his cellular and paused a second before dialing.

"Brad? This is unexpected. I was actually planning on reaching out to you. Is everything alright?" Fairbanks hummed on the line.

"I'm sorry to bother you, but you said anything at all."

"I did. What can I do for you?"

"What can you tell me about the senator?"

"Give me a second here." Barnes could hear background voices, some shuffling through the line and then the sound of a door shutting. . .quiet. "Sorry about that I needed to get to a more secure area to talk. He's not all that popular with the press, but his constituents seem to love him. He was just re-elected. You're not thinking he's involved are you? It was his kid that was killed, right?"

"I'm gathering information, thought you might know more about him than a background check would reveal. You're in the circle."

"I don't know much but what I do know is that he's a powerful man, very connected. He's also considered a little aggressive. Most avoid him and few stand their ground in his path. They call him Winslow the Water Buffalo. Don't let that leak, I've got a career to protect." He laughed.

"Well, I guess that helps a little." Barnes re-directed. "You were going to reach out to me, you said?"

"Brad, this is sensitive, and we never talked." Fairbanks was almost whispering. "I've got a bead on the illegal involved in Patricia's accident. I'll get you the info soon, I owe that to you and Patricia."

"Can we bring him back?" The detective's enthusiasm was hard to keep tempered.

"I'll be out of the country for about a week. We'll talk when I get back. I'm trying to help and counting on your complete secrecy until then. No one can even know we spoke." Fairbanks didn't wait for a response and clicked off.

CHAPTER 34

She woke up to the sound of the scavenging seagulls and mammoth waves pounding the rocky shoreline at the bottom of the cliffs. The sun hadn't yet cleared the mountains to the east. Behind her, the slight rim of daylight promised some warmth would soon come on the morning air. But she wasn't ready yet to come out of hiding. Her defenses were still on high alert. It had been hours—she wasn't sure how many. She was still a little fuzzy from the night before when she pulled the palm fronds over her but was much more clear-headed now.

She peeked out through the leaves, sensitive to every sound, and looked around as much as she could. *How long should I stay put?* she wondered. Her anxiety was still peaking despite the night's rest. Her wrists hurt from the tie wraps. She found a small rock and rubbed the plastic against it until it broke, free at last.

Slowly, she moved out of the leafy cover and stood behind the trunk of a large palm tree, surveying the area. There was no one within sight. The commercial area appeared deserted, as did the trail leading to the lighthouse.

Treacherous was the only way she could describe the path that thinned at the most dangerous part of the trek up ahead. Iron bars had been installed as a barrier to prevent people from falling over the cliff's edge, but had almost all rotted away. It appeared to her that she might have dodged a bullet by not continuing there the night before.

She found the fork where the trail split, avoided the cliffs, and ran down to the beach below. Heading back to the commercial complex was not an option, so the sandy path to the beach it was.

The gown she wore did little to cover her, and she figured she must look a little like an escaped mental patient. She folded her arms across her chest to keep warm and hiked the rest of the way to the huge cove and public area below.

On the beach ahead of her, a young woman danced in the sand, chasing the waves, tiptoeing through the wet muck at the water's edge. Her large-brimmed hat covered her bouncy auburn hair and her fancy peach-patterned sun dress plumed as she twirled.

The woman seemed so free—a feeling that was very foreign to Reagan right now. But she also seemed happy...happy and safe. The teen moved toward her until the young woman saw her and stopped twirling. She seemed stunned at the young girl's presence as if she was staring at a ghost.

"Oh, my..." the woman cried out. "Owen," she yelled. "Help."

An older man sat up and watched as the woman grabbed a huge beach towel and headed toward the youngster. She wrapped the towel around her like a blanket and led her to where they were sitting. "Are you alright, honey?" the young woman asked. "You look pekid."

The older man appeared a bit disconnected.

"Owen, can you get her something to drink?"

He brought her a cold bottle of water from their cooler and a few crackers with cheese.

Reagan took the food and collapsed in the sand to cry.

The woman wrapped her arms around her and motioned for another beach towel, which she pulled over her shoulders.

"It's okay, honey, you're safe here," she consoled. "Are you hurt?"

"No," Reagan looked over her shoulders, gobbling up the crackers. "Just a little scared."

"Oh, you poor thing," the woman soothed. "We'll protect you. You'll be safe with us. I'm Corrina, and this is my husband, Doctor Owen Nichols."

The doctor gave her a little wave and a weak smile.

"Do you want some more to drink? Perhaps some more food?"

Reagan nodded, and Nichols handed over more crackers and cheese.

"Owen, get your phone," Corrina requested, turning her attention back to the girl. "Is there someone we can call for you, your mother or father, or maybe some friends? Do you want to tell us what happened?"

She could barely piece a sentence together between sobs. "I-I don't know. I thought I was in a hospital or psychiatric ward. I couldn't remember anything. They told me my mom was gone. I thought I was somehow responsible, that I'd hurt her."

"Oh, you poor thing, you must be terrified," Corrina soothed trying to dredge up any memory of her mother, but couldn't.

"Then I remembered I was kidnapped and they brought me here," Reagan started. "But I got away and ran. It was so dark, the pavement hurt my feet. They were chasing me, looking for me, but I hid, and they finally left...I was so frightened. I want to call my mom," she cried again.

"Of course, honey." Corrina took the phone from her reluctant husband and wondered if she was on the level. "What's the number?"

"I don't know." She looked confused. "It's programmed into my phone, and I don't have it. He took it and I can't remember the number." The tears kept coming.

"Who took it, honey?"

"That man...with the empty eyes...big, dark...empty eyes." She couldn't control the sobbing.

"It's okay, we'll help you. Owen," she pleaded. "What can we do?"

"Well, she appears to have a mild case of exposure from the cold and is in a state of shock," he surmised. "Let's get her to the clinic to clean her up, get her some fluids, and stabilize her while we figure out how to reach her parents."

"Okay, honey. Is that alright with you?" Corrina consoled her with another hug.

"I'm so cold and scared." She buried her head against Corrina's shoulder.

Minutes later, they had piled all of their belongings into the silver Mercedes and were headed toward the clinic. Corrina sat in the back seat with Reagan while they navigated the ride along the coast.

"Owen, we should call the police. We need to get someone looking into this. They'll know what to do," Corrina suggested from the back seat.

"Of course, dear," Nichols responded. "As soon as we get there. But let's get this young lady clean, safe, and warm first. After that, I'm sure the police will locate her family and get them reconnected. Everything is going to work out just fine." He smiled at his wife convincingly in the rearview mirror.

CHAPTER 35

S he finally started to relax once they arrived at the clinic. The doctor had a nurse look her over and attend to some of the small wounds and scrapes she had picked up, especially on her worn feet. Reagan took a warm shower, and they hooked up an IV to give her some much-needed fluids. They put her on a bed, brought her some more food, and switched the TV on while she rested.

Doctor Nichols and Corrina were back to check on her again once she was settled. "How are you feeling, Reagan?" Nichols asked.

Corrina's warm smile was comforting. "Hey there, honey. Your skin color has returned. You look so pretty."

"Much better," she said. "Can we call my mom now? I know she's worried."

"Of course, she is, sweetie. Any mom would be..." Corrina soothed.

"It's worse than that. The last time we saw each other, we were fighting. She was so mad at me. I said some mean things and left."

Corrina's words were reinforcing. "Listen, honey, trust me on this. Mom is going to forgive you and apologize, and you'll both be close again. My heart melts for you."

Tears welled in Reagan's eyes. "Do you really think so? She was so angry with me."

"Honey, I guarantee it!" Corrina bent down and hugged her.

The doctor interrupted, "I've made a call to the police station and a detective friend of mine is on his way to get your statement and personal information so he can find your mom and get her here."

"Oh, thank you, thank you. You two have been so good to me," Reagan oozed with gratitude. "I'll never be able to repay you."

"Getting you back home will be all the compensation I need." Corrina smiled beautifully.

They left her to rest, and she drifted off for a couple of hours. When she woke, the TV was still on, droning with the national news. She used the remote control to turn it off and wondered how she could get some food. Her appetite was back with a vengeance.

She could hear some talking going on in the hallway but couldn't make out the details.

"Yes, I'm well aware of the situation. That's why I called you." The doctor kept his voice low. Though the hallway was empty, he was careful. "Look, I don't know how it happened, but some people are not affected by morphine. It's a physiological condition. Their bodies do not synthesize the opiate. She must've been able to shake off the effects and escaped." He was getting uncomfortable there in the clinic and needed to get off the phone. "We can talk more when you get here. See you in 10 minutes."

He took a little time to compose himself, manufactured some professionalism, and headed to see his young patient.

She heard the faint knock on the door. "Reagan, it's Doctor Nichols. May I come in?"

"Of course, Doctor, you'd better be armed with some munchies though," she laughed.

"Well, that's certainly a good sign, both your hunger and your sense of humor have returned."

"Yes, I know. I'm feeling so much more like myself." She almost bubbled with joy. "Where's Corrina?"

"Oh, she went home to pick out some clothes for you. We can't have your mom taking a pretty little thing like you home in that hospital gown, now, can we?"

"Oh, you reached my mom. Is she on her way here? Now?" Reagan's excitement was uncontainable.

"No, not just yet. But the detective is on his way here. As a matter of fact, I was just speaking with him. He's very anxious to get this cleared up." Nichols adjusted her IV bag.

"I can't wait to get home. I don't even know how long I've been gone. What day is it?" she asked.

"It's Monday, November 14th," he answered, listening to the beeping monitors.

"No way, it's been more than a month." She became agitated, and fear returned to her eyes. "I don't remember any of it."

"Easy now, Reagan," Nichols calmed. "The detective will be here soon, and you can tell him everything. It's almost all over."

"I just want to go home." A sad look washed across her face.

Nichols tried to redirect her anxiety. He asked about her pets and school and her friends, and the brief chat seemed genuine when a head peeked around the room divider.

"Well, it's about time," Nichols announced.

Reagan sat up, ready to get things moving.

"Honey, this is my friend, the detective I told you about. He's here to get your information and hear all about your adventure." They shook hands.

"Reagan, is that right?" he asked in a friendly voice.

"Yes, hello," she answered awkwardly.

The detective held up a photo on printed paper. "This wouldn't be you, would it?" He smiled.

"Oh no. Am I on the wanted list?" Her mouth opened in horror.

"Well, you are on a wanted list of sorts, yes." He laughed. "This is a missing person's picture filed by a detective down in L.A." He extended his hand in greeting. "I'm Detective Grimes..."

CHAPTER 36

The rain had intensified during the breakfast with the councilman, and Barnes darted to the Crown Vic to avoid getting drenched. He lingered in the front seat, watching the trails of droplets streaming down the windshield, gathering his thoughts. The doll-like hostess was haunting him and then his thoughts drifted to Patricia—the accident. *Get to the point*, she'd said. It was broken like she was trying to formulate a thought, but maybe it was literal.

Get to the point?
Rocky Point.

A million things crashed through his head as he sat there. Time stood still and his mind turned to the clues and connections. It seemed as if every raindrop that pelted the car's roof was another line of thought, another new direction, a new possibility.

Jim's concern seemed genuine, but given the circumstances, he wasn't sure who to trust. He remembered Patricia telling him that the main office had shut down her investigation into a missing girl. The case he had handed her. Was the councilman now trying to shut down this investigation? *No, we've known each other too long, there's no way he's involved.*

He'd barely finished the thought when his phone chimed. He answered on the second ring. "Colt, what's up?"

"You are coming in today, right?"

"Yeah, I'm sorry, I had to meet with the councilman this morning. He's getting very antsy," Barnes explained. "I'm on my way in now."

"Uh, make it quick, will ya?"

"Everything okay? You sound funny."

"Yes, fine, we've just got a lot to do, that's all. See you in a few, right?" The line went dead.

Barnes continued processing his encounter with Councilman Meyer, finally ruling out any nefarious intention. *He probably needs this case closed as quickly as possible. The community is likely restless, that's all,* he thought.

The station wasn't too far away, but the weather had wreaked havoc on the commute. The gutters overflowed with water and the higher-than-normal tides saw ocean water pushing up through the sewer manholes. Increased winds had picked up and palm tree fronds littered the streets.

When an accident in front of him threatened to stop traffic, he decided to pull off the main road and use the side roads to cut the trip time.

The old detective pulled into the yard about 20 minutes after hanging up with his partner. He passed through the lobby, down the hall past the copiers and printers, realizing they weren't as loud without a hangover. He finally entered into the swamp—what Colton had recently nicknamed the detective's office space.

Colton was sitting opposite a tall man who looked as if he'd spent his entire life in a gym. His crew cut harkened to another era, a Johnny Unitas style. He had a barrel chest and arms that filled out the entire sleeve of his dark blue sport coat.

"Brad." Colton caught the movement as he entered. "This here is agent Trent. He's come a long way to see us."

The enormous relic of a man pulled out his badge and wallet, displaying his ID. "Hello, Detective Barnes. The man behind me is Agent Mills, we're with the justice department out of DC. I'm Garrett Trent, SAC."

"Special Agent in Charge?" Barnes guessed.

"Yes, Mr. Barnes, Special Circumstances Unit." They shook hands.

"Well, that clears up some things."

Noble looked a little confused, "Brad?"

"Remember when I told you I thought we'd stumbled onto something big? Well, we're about to get the lay of the land, Colt." Barnes stuck a fresh toothpick between his teeth and thought briefly before launching into it. "Perhaps we should move to the conference room?"

"Wherever you feel best," Agent Trent smiled. "Lead the way."

"Mind if I grab a coffee first?" Barnes requested.

"Not at all."

Barnes waited for everyone to be seated before speaking. "So, Sutherland was yours?" the detective assumed.

"Yup. Michael Brown was his real name. Former Army ranger. We got the alert when you ran his tags... obviously our system is sophisticated. He was due to come in for his renewal review. Undercover cases have to be approved every six months, and this op was scheduled to close. He'd already been in the field for a year and a half and that's six months more than like to be operational. But we lost contact about a week before the murders."

"Sorry for the loss." Barnes was empathetic. "Might not mean much to you, but all records indicate your guy was stand up."

"Appreciate that. You mentioned getting the lay of the land? You mind giving us what you have first?"

He looked at his partner, took a deep breath, and began, "Well, your visit cemented some thoughts I had."

"How's that?" Agent Mills responded.

"I know DOJ-sensitive circumstances are only involved if there is a political angle. Possible misconduct by an elected or appointed official. That confirms my thoughts and places the senator directly in the crosshairs," Barnes supposed.

"Go on."

"But he's only part of the picture. You're after something bigger. You want his operation, and you were trying to get to all of the tentacles before the squid ditched it and left it somewhat intact or operational."

"Interesting metaphor," Trent scowled.

"I got some help from an anonymous tip on the senator's kid. He'd been accused of some activity—allegedly, of course—that forced the closure of his practice in Connecticut."

"We're aware," Trent waited.

"Nothing in the background, though, right, Colt?" Barnes asked without even looking at his partner.

"Not even a traffic ticket," Colt responded.

"We figured that had to be the senator that cleaned that mess up. Things got a little interesting when we went through the senator's son's files. The son was seeing a patient, a deceased patient," Barnes continued.

"Significance?" Trent steepled his fingers, watching as Barnes paced the room.

"The dead wife of Doctor Owen Nichols. He was coincidentally the only witness to the double homicide that claimed the senator's son and your guys' lives." Barnes paused briefly.

"I'll need that information, if you don't mind?" Mills interjected.

Barnes motioned for Colt to make a note.

"Are you saying the old guy, the doctor, killed these two out there on the beach?" Trent appeared confused.

Barnes circled the table and took a long sip of his coffee. "I wasn't sure at first. I mean, how could an old guy take out two guys half his age? But during the autopsy, our coroner mentioned that the wound appeared almost surgical in nature. It went straight to the heart, bypassed all ribs, cartilage, etc. It was a precision strike, he called it. Seems to me that only one of those three was capable of that."

"I can see the strike being precise as a cause for calling the doctor in question, but I agree, I'm still confused about how he could overpower the two men at his age?"

"Questions for when I get back to the doctor's house." Barnes went on, "You see, my partner asked a great question after interviewing the doc the other day. Colt thought he had admitted to providing his wife with the medication that led to her suicide."

"I remember that," Colt added.

"In fact, what was said was quite different…'Where do you think she got the meds…?'"

"But the doc was distraught, guilty even. He must've provided that medication," Colt returned.

"When we reviewed the therapist's patient list, the doc's wife came up. I believe that the senator's son provided the medication and Nichols held Mason responsible, even though she made the choice to take her own life. My contention was that the doc was not down at the beach reminiscing over the photo of his wife but building his courage. I think he called the therapist there specifically to confront him. Maybe not to kill him, perhaps to threaten him, maybe get him to confess, but something changed."

"So, what was Sutherland, sorry, Mike Brown doing there?" Colt added.

"Yeah, there's just no way the old doctor took out a former ranger," Trent argued.

"I haven't got an answer for that yet. But I think some of that may have been answered by Miss Sable. Were you gentlemen aware that Mr. Brown was gay?" Barnes quizzed.

"Don't ask, don't tell," Mills was quick to respond.

"I think possibly there was a relationship between him and the senator's son, or maybe they were just friends, but my guess is that your guy was there to protect Mason Walker."

"When did you piece all of this together? How long have you been holding out on me?" Colt was a bit perturbed.

"Actually, since breakfast. With the councilman this morning," Barnes stated. "There was a hostess, cute little thing, couldn't have been more than 17 years old. She smiled at me and reminded me of a missing persons case I had given to my wife before she passed." Barnes paused and fought back some emotion.

The other three waited patiently.

The elder detective sipped at his coffee again. "She had bright red hair, which she wore in pigtails, soft white skin with freckles, and this little gap between her teeth." He paused, looking for a word that eluded him. She looked a little like a Raggedy Ann doll or something, like she was in costume. It struck me as…what was it, Colt, that Kayleigh, the therapist's assistant called it?

"Cosplay?" he replied, glad to contribute. "It's costume and role-playing like she said the senator's kid liked to do."

"Right." Barnes shook his hands to illustrate his frustration with the thinking process. "It triggered something that had been gnawing at me, pulling on my subconscious. My wife, in her dying moments, talked about a case with this missing girl and said the FBI had hard closed the case even though she thought she was making progress. She'd found similar reports. The perpetrator was always dressed in uniform. Something safe, benign, like a policeman, military...or priest."

Colt made the instant connection. "Like some of the costumes in the therapist's closet..."

"Bingo, partner." Barnes slapped the table. "That's why we're here, isn't it, gentlemen? This isn't about a simple murder, a crime of passion. No, it's much bigger than that, why else would you have an undercover agent here, right?"

The agents exchanged a quick look.

"This is about human trafficking, a ring that has far-reaching implications and it seems the senator is at the head of the snake. It was his son who was picking these young, defenseless victims off the street and bringing them here, right? That's why the DOJ and the Sensitive Operations Unit are involved. My wife could've stopped it...If the FBI had only listened"

Agent Trent stood and made direct eye contact with the detective who had ranted so passionately. "I'm sorry you didn't know, Detective Barnes. But your wife is precisely the reason we are here, the reason for this case. It was her dogged persistence that brought this mess to my doorstep. It was her second attempt to bring attention to this case. She wouldn't let it go. And it is a tragedy that she cannot be here to see what you have accomplished. We intend to honor her memory. In doing so, we are going to let you bring this home and offer you every resource that we have at our disposal."

"Patricia brought this to you, and you couldn't tell me?" Barnes was beside himself. He remembered the last brief discussion with Fairbanks and wondered if everything in the DOJ was so secretive that even they didn't share intel.

"Detective, until you ran those tags, we had an active undercover investigation. Our agent may have gone so deep that he couldn't get the word out. You must understand the sensitivity of this operation. The senator's son was the 'bottom', you just gave us that. He's the intermediary between the asset and the owner. He is easily tied by your investigation to his father."

"Then this should be a wrap, let's go grab this dirtbag and shut this operation down," Barnes argued.

"It's not that simple, Detective."

"Not that simple?" Noble asked, confused. "I don't understand. What's the problem?"

"The big problem is that they don't have his direct fingerprints on this," Barnes realized. "He has plausible deniability where his son is concerned. If they storm in, he can still walk away clean, or at least clean enough. He'll make himself appear to be the victim in all of this and actually play the sympathy card."

Trent summed it up. "That's correct, Detective. He is a United States senator with friends in high places. His sphere of influence is wide-ranging. This will be a tremendous negative reflection on our government at a time when our nation's trust is at an all-time low. I'm sure you felt the tension following the contested election. Corruption in high office is crippling to our nation, its economy and judicial system. If this is not handled correctly, it could be catastrophic. We have to have all of our ducks in a row, evidentiary, legally, and without doubt."

Barnes was staring into space, processing the new information about his dead wife. He felt as if he'd been hit by a wrecking ball.

"Detectives, I need to get to the point here," Trent spoke loudly.

'*Get to the point.*' Barnes heard it again in Patricia's voice.

"Your wife thought she was onto something and took a great risk. To be completely clear, this case is so sensitive that the only people who are aware of this information are in this room. If you want to keep working on this, it needs to stay that way."

"Of course, Agent Trent," Barnes re-engaged. "You have my word."

"Mine too," Colt added.

"Can you show us what you have now?"

Trent flopped a briefcase on the table and pulled out some documents. There were pictures of seven other young girls, all missing persons cases. He unfolded a large map that had interlocking circles drawn out over it. "This is some of what your wife handed to us."

Barnes and Noble stared at the map, digesting the information.

"Partner?" Colt queried.

"It's the other missing persons cases she'd tracked that had the same MO. All in California, all near the coast."

"That's right, Detective. She'd drawn a 100-mile circle from each incident and the overlapping diameter put Rocky Point near the epicenter, the only city that was close," Agent Trent clarified.

She was trying to guide me here, Barnes reconciled. "Why wasn't I informed? You must've known I'd been brought into the case; you knew about the homicides on the beach? This was my wife, for the love of God!"

Noble was feeling the tension rise and becoming increasingly uncomfortable.

"We had a missing agent, an active case investigation, and to reiterate, there are two people in the DOJ aware of this— myself and Agent Mills. As I stated, it needed to stay that way. We wanted to see what you were able to put together once the murder investigation commenced without bringing in the Cavalry and potentially alerting the senator. It was important that he felt he still controlled the playing field."

Barnes mulled over the new information as Agent Mills tossed another document on the table.

"I recognize this. It's a copy of the email tip I got from the USER@Connpublib email address. How did you get this?"

"It was sent by another UCA who was posing as the senator's assistant."

"Do we have enough now?" Noble asked.

"No, kid. Everything we have would still be considered circumstantial. Taking him in now would get things tied up in litigation and his lawyers and political record would probably wipe him clean."

"That's correct but you are still in a position to get what we need directly on the senator. Because of that and because of your relationship with Patricia, I'm giving you the opportunity to bring this home. I have only the highest level of respect for her principles and courage. I'm deeply sorry for your loss, but I'm counting on you to honor her memory and that of Michael Brown in this investigation. Are we clear?"

"Clear," both Colt and Barnes confirmed.

"Fantastic." Agent Mills tossed two cellular phones on the conference table. "Now, let's sit and talk about the communication trails, timing, and methods. We need to be in the loop…"

CHAPTER 37

Barnes was exhausted after the meeting with the DOJ agents. It was a lot to take in and his mind was still spinning. The new information and his wife's connection to the case had spiked his energy, but he was crashing hard when he pulled away for the station house.

The drive up the coast took him past Rose's Diner, where he'd met with the councilman for breakfast. The powerful beam from the lighthouse flashed across the highway as it turned repeatedly, warning ships to stray from the rocky shore and cliffs. Lingering at the intersection, he waited for the traffic signal to turn green and stared ahead into the blank, crisp night. The strong white beam continued to pass across his face, reflecting off his windshield, each time filling the interior of the car before giving way to the red flood of the stoplight.

He wondered how many sailors that beacon had saved in all the years it'd been there. Then in the contradiction, he thought about Colton and his 'jumpers' and how many lives had been lost off of the platform plunging into the cold, dark waters over 100 feet below. He recalled telling Colton about his 'healthy respect' for heights, but the truth was, he hated them. He didn't like air travel, either. That's one reason they'd always used the rail system back in school.

The Crown Victoria pulled into the beach parking lot close to where old Doc Nichols' Mercedes was parked that morning, and Barnes turned his thoughts to the case. He liked to isolate when he had heavy thinking to do. *How were they going to definitively link the senator to his son's actions? What was the real connection between Sutherland and the therapist? Who were the goons that stormed in on Kayleigh? Would they return? Why isn't this adding up? Still so many answers to find, so many missing pieces.*

He let his mind roam, hoping that the freedom of thought would help sort things out and put the pieces together. Outside, the storm had slowed in terms of moisture but he was certain more was on the way. He watched the lightning, observed the flashing of the sky, and counted, waiting for the thunder's boom, just the way he'd seen in a movie years before.

He noted that the time between the flashing and the sound was shrinking, which told him rain was getting closer, and the winds were picking up. The storm would soon pound the coastal town again. It might wash away the silt and dust from the streets, but the dirt of what happened here was not yet ready to leave.

He tracked with the beam from the lighthouse as it toured the surface of the ocean, over the sand and parking lot, mesmerized by its hypnotic rhythm. He reclined the driver's seat and turned on the heater at the low setting, just enough to keep the windows clear and provide a little warmth. He started looking at the scene at the beach with fresh eyes. *What if things were not as they appeared? What if the doc is more involved than we think? Was he looking for more than revenge for his wife? Who else has dirt on their hands? I need to get back to the doc's house and ask some more questions.*

Half an hour passed and then a small car drove into the lot. It took a space at the far end of the parking area, near the trailhead that led to the lighthouse.

He watched as a young woman got out and made her way up the path. Instantly, the thought of Colton's 'jumpers' raced through his head. The car door opened and he hopped out, calling at her, but the winds were stronger now and he couldn't yell loud enough to get her attention. There was a flashlight under his seat. He grabbed it, pointed it toward the trail, and hit the button...nothing. He tossed it back onto the seat in frustration, closed the door, and started after her.

Why on earth would anyone choose to go out this way? the thought blinked. He tried screaming again, but the gale-force winds just knocked his voice down. It was as if he was moving in slow motion. He shielded his face with a hand, trying to keep her in sight as the rain finally reached the coast. The beacon light circled again and he saw her reaching the top. There was a pause as if perhaps she was considering her decision.

His breathing became labored and he pressed harder, running now, slipping as the sand and dirt packed on the trail turned muddy. To improve his footing, he stepped off the path and used the plants, grass, and whatever vegetation was available. He looked up again and she was gone. *I guess she made up her mind.*

The distance between them had closed. Somehow, with her pause and his running, he'd managed to close the gap. He reached the top and caught sight of her again, edging along the narrow part of the trail where the iron railing was rusting away. He broke into a sprint, calling out. But it was no use. The winds coming in off the bluff and the crashing of the mammoth waves below made it impossible for her to hear him. *Would she stop anyway?* he wondered.

With only 50 feet separating them, she slipped and fell, sliding over the edge. She reached out for the railing and caught a broken piece of it just before going over. Barnes was there an instant later, and despite his gripping fear, he crawled on his stomach, made it to the rail, and extended his arm to her. He clasped her hand as it slid from the railing and kept her from falling into the rocks and crashing waves below. She looked up at him with her beautiful blue eyes and the gold flecks sparkled as they had that day under the gazebo. There was that smile again—Patricia.

"You have to let me go…"

He woke up yelling, "I'll never let you go!" and pounded at the car's ceiling until his knuckles puffed with blood. His scream echoed in the dark, wet night.

CHAPTER 38

It was still pitch dark in the early morning hours. Colton was waiting when Barnes pulled in to pick him up at the station. He'd received the text after midnight, after the dream in the parking lot. "You look beat, partner."

"Yeah, rough night." Barnes ran his hand through his hair and then readjusted the toothpick. "But we gotta move fast and I want to ask the doc a few more questions."

"You sure you don't wanna get some rest first? Go in with a fresh mind?"

"Not getting a lot of rest these days." Barnes pulled out into traffic and headed toward the doc's house. He rubbed at the bags under his eyes. "The dreams are killing me."

"Had another one, huh?" Noble clicked on his seatbelt.

Barnes thought for a minute before answering. "Yeah, but this one had a kick to it. A real smash-bang ending."

Noble gave it space to breathe. "You want to talk about it?"

"No, I wanna ask Nichols some questions and put this to bed." Barnes laughed maniacally. "Then I want to get the most

powerful tranquilizer they make and take a long winter's nap."
He tapped at his noggin.

"You losing it, partner?" Noble asked.

Barnes sighed. "No, it's just funny sometimes how the human mind works."

"If you say so." Noble hesitated, "You're okay to drive, right?"

"I'm fine, kid."

"Speaking of which, I got the report on the car last night." Noble smiled.

"You plan on sharing at some point?"

"Someone cut the brake line, must've snuck in while we were talking to the doc. Not clean, so it took a while to bleed the fluid."

"Well, I guess that clears up that little mystery," Barnes hissed.

"If it doesn't, this'll bring some sure clarity." He paused.

Barnes looked at him before turning up Canyon Drive.

"They bugged the car. Someone's been listening to us. Don't know how long, but they've been listening."

Barnes looked out the windshield at the sky as he assimilated the new info. *Is this storm ever going to end?*

"I can put a call into Trent to see if it was them. Could be that they wanted to know what we knew and when we knew it," Colt suggested.

"No need. It was the senator or that agent, Wright."

"How do you know that?"

"Trent didn't even know they lost an agent until we ran those dog tags. The timing doesn't work," Barnes summed.

"Crap, of course," Noble agreed.

"We've really got to get to the doc fast. They're gonna figure that we know enough to be dangerous. I'm positive they are in mop-up mode now. Time is of the essence."

"If I'm reading you right and the doc is involved, then it's safe to say his life is in danger also?" Noble reasoned.

"You think I wanted to get out here this early just to gab?" Barnes asked sarcastically.

CHAPTER 39

This drive up the canyon to Doc Nichols' place was far more uneventful than their last drive down. Clouds threatened rain, but the skies never followed through on the promise.

"So, they bugged the vehicle?" Barnes thought out loud. "That gives the attempts on our lives substantiation."

"Yeah, I suppose they'd have known we moved past the crime of passion or jealousy angle and would keep on digging."

"So, they had to send a message." Barnes played it out. "The bar incident."

"When that didn't work?"

"The only way to buy time and get us off their tails was to injure or kill us." He moved his toothpick with his tongue.

"The cut brake line?" Noble chimed.

"Yeah, the cut brake line. It had to look like an accident or it would be too obvious, and the feds would be called in. But this time, they wanted us erased."

"They must be shitting themselves now, then?" Noble laughed. "They have to figure we know something and haven't been able to stop us. Maybe more than they expect."

The Crown Victoria fought a strong crosswind before making the climb up the mountain and into the drive of the relocated castle. Barnes cut the engine and the tires crunched and popped on the loose gravel covering the driveway as they coasted to a quiet stop, using the tremendous fountain to shield them from view.

No lights were on in the home, but from his position, Barnes could tell that the front door was ajar. "Weapons," he whispered, and they exited the car without closing the doors to avoid announcing their arrival. With their Glock 357 sigs in hand, they approached the residence in cover and conceal formation.

There was no resistance, and they made it to the door without incidence. Barnes pushed it slightly and slowly looked in. He finally kicked the door open, waving Noble past him. Colton turned on his small flashlight and cleared the foyer and hallway while Barnes targeted the stairs. Once checked, they moved deeper into the room.

It was almost pitch dark and their eyes had not yet acclimated to the new surroundings. There was no movement, but they heard a 'tink' from the piano. Noble trained his light and weapon in the direction of the tone. Barnes followed suit.

"There's no need for gunplay, Detectives." Nichols' scratchy voice hummed a melody as he caught their reflections in the in a mirror.

"Let me see your hands, now!" Barnes ordered, trying to place the tune.

Nichols lifted them into the air to show he was unarmed.

"Am I a suspect?"

"Just being careful. Are you okay?" Barnes queried. "We came out to talk and noticed the door was open…"

"I'm just fine, Detectives. But you're too late." He 'plinked' a couple more keys on the piano.

"Too late?" Barnes holstered his weapon. "What are we too late for?"

"Yeah, Doc, we just came out to check on you again, that's all." Noble read Barnes' hand motions and began to circle around the room toward the doctor.

"Yes, of course you did." He chuckled. "I managed to duck them, but they left just before you arrived." Nichols returned to humming the melody.

Barnes recognized the tune. *Ashes, ashes, we all fall down.* A chill ran the length of his spine. "Who left?"

Colton tripped on the leg of the end table.

"I'd prefer you gentlemen to keep your distance if you want my cooperation, thank you." He raised his hands and slammed them in a dramatic harmonic minor chord on the keyboard. "You'll need it to get what you're after."

Barnes waved his partner off. "Who left?" he asked again.

"The men you seek." Nichols hummed again, getting louder. "Come now, you must've figured it out, Detective?"

"I've figured out a lot, but not all of it." Barnes began, "I know that the senator is running a trafficking ring right here in Rocky Point. I know that Mason was the 'bottom'. He acquired the victims, brought them here, where they were beaten, threatened, addicted to drugs, or physically abused until they were broken. Indoctrinated into the system. Unable to break free."

The old doctor kept humming, undaunted. "Congratulations, Detective."

Barnes' mind was twisting in thought. *Right here in Rocky Point. Not a big city or a large metropolitan district, but a small, quaint beach town. Keeping everything under the radar, almost invisible.* He became agitated when he remembered. *I didn't listen. Get to the point,* Patricia said. He was sure he'd heard her voice. *Listen and you will hear.*

The doc continued drumming the piano keys. "If you are so certain, why haven't you apprehended this villain?"

"The arrest warrants have been issued," Barnes replied, pulling out his soggy toothpick, ready for a fresh replacement. "It's just a matter of time before we take this thing down."

Nichols just continued to tinker with the piano keyboard. "You won't get to him. He's too big. He can fix anything, clean up any mess, make it go away. You don't know what you're up against."

"Is that right? Is he going to clean your mess, too? We know you were at the beach that morning, but I do not believe you were reminiscing. You were planning on confronting Corrina's therapist. We discovered he was treating her for depression. You failed to disclose that on the last visit."

"You couldn't expect me to just hand you the keys to the car..." Plink, plunk. "But it wasn't depression, Detective. Oh, he convinced her it was. Sometimes the smallest ripple can turn into a tsunami."

"Not sure I follow you, Doc."

"No, you couldn't know. Corrina was not her real name. She came here years ago; Mason did a good job fixing her."

"Fixing her, Doc?"

"Yes, Mason was a remarkable hypnotist and his fascination with brainwashing, or mind-bending as he called it, made him quite useful."

Son of a...Menticide, it clicked. Barnes was connecting the dots.

"Everything was fine until a chance encounter at a local gas station with the security guard at the dance club fractured her thinking. She thought she was losing her mind, remembering things long hidden."

"So, you sent her back to see Mason?" Barnes suggested.

"Yes, to re-program her, but she was no longer receptive and became problematic...headaches, anxiety, night terrors."

"The records indicate that he gave her a prescription. It was the medication he had prescribed that she used to kill herself, wasn't it? And you held him responsible? You wanted him to own that."

"Ta-da!" Nichols pounded on the piano. "Another piece of the puzzle falls into place. Took you a while, but you got there." Plink, tink.

"What I couldn't understand for the longest time was what your intentions were. I don't think that you meant to kill him. You couldn't possibly have thought you could overpower Walker?"

"No, certainly not at first, and when his partner showed up with him, it complicated things." The doc hummed quietly. "But then, I didn't know the whole story yet."

"You knew he prescribed her drugs…the drugs she used to overdose?" Barnes recounted.

Noble was beginning to get creeped out by the strange humming and the untimely keyboard hits. He slipped onto one of the French chairs.

"Yes, but it was then that Mason informed me that it was all my fault. That I had killed her." The doc stopped tinking and humming and took a deep breath.

"You killed her?" Barnes questioned. "But you sent her to the therapist, you said so yourself."

"Indeed, but it seems that during one of her sessions, she confided in Mason her suspicions about me." Nichols resumed the piano play.

"I've had my own suspicions," Barnes announced. "I was digging into the senator's background and ran across information on his father. Family history, political background, and pictures, of course. Pictures like the one on your mantle."

Colton shot his partner a look.

"Very good, Detective." He struck another key. "You don't miss a thing."

"That tied you to this whole mess but it doesn't explain why she talked to the therapist about you, or why you killed him?"

"Let's take him in, Brad." Noble got up from the chair. "This is creepy."

"If you try to take me in, I assure you, you'll lose my cooperation." Nichols sat straight.

There was a long pause between them that Barnes used to signify that there was no movement to arrest the doc.

"You're saying that she talked to Mason about you?" Barnes was processing.

"I thought you had this piece, Detective." Nichols smiled at no one.

Barnes' silence was lengthy. "She found out that you were involved. It has to be?" he reasoned.

"Pop goes the weasel." Nichols followed the piano notes. "A mistake, a physiological anomaly. You see, it takes many parts to make a machine such as this operate efficiently. People with a specific skill, position of influence or power. Mine was medicinal, but things occur. A girl. A beautiful young girl that would have been sold internationally for hundreds of thousands or more. She escaped, and the results could've been dire." Plink, plink.

Barnes tossed another toothpick on the floor.

"She was recovered, of course, and we temporarily averted disaster. Just appeared on the beach right in front of us on one of those days I told you about when I sat in the ambulance that cold morning. Corrina found her, took to her rather quickly, wanted to, needed to help her because no one had helped Corrina when she needed it." He played a string of notes. *The worms crawl in, the worms crawl out...*

"Doc, the music, really?" Noble exchanged looks with his partner and shifted uncomfortably in the chair.

"Oh, these old tunes." He laughed. "I used to play them for the kids at the clinic. Aren't they a delight?"

"What happened with the girl?" Barnes redirected.

"We brought the girl to the clinic, cleaned her up. Corrina made me call the police to help find her family. Later, she went to visit the detective in care of the case. She wanted to check on the girl, make sure she was okay and didn't need anything. That was my Corrina, always so loving."

"But the girl never made it home, did she? You couldn't allow that to happen. It would bring a focus to your operation. You might have to suspend business, and that means lost revenue," Barnes twisted.

"You are on the right trail, Detective." Nichols' shaking hands clapped.

"So, you killed her?" Barnes supposed.

He plinked the keyboard with sour notes. "Oh, wrong answer, Mr. Barnes."

"She was still alive…she is still alive? And, somehow, Corrina figured?" the detective guessed.

"Row, row, row your boat…" Nichols played along.

"Corrina told Mason in confidence during her sessions," Barnes was piecing things together. "The detective was stonewalling her with the information on the girl's family."

"Mason told her she was imagining things and prescribed her anti-psychotics and sleeping pill tranquilizers. He purposely dosed her incorrectly." Nichols raged. "It was not a suicide, it was murder."

"Oh, shit," Colton inadvertently blurted.

"Yes, oh shit," the doctor giggled like a scary clown. "An eye for an eye."

But how? Barnes was rebuilding the beach crime scene in his mind.

"You were right, Brad. Walker was trying to get away," Noble recalled.

"You couldn't have overpowered those two men," Barnes spoke the obvious.

*The monkey chased the weasel...*plink, plink. "No, I could not out muscle them. But when Mason admitted to killing Corrina, his friend went crazy. He talked as if he knew her. He said he was an undercover agent and tried to arrest us both."

"He was the bouncer who helped your wife at the strip club," Barnes informed.

"Sutherland had enough, evidently," Noble said.

"Mason panicked and threw a can of beer at him, breaking his nose. There was blood everywhere. He went down like a sack of potatoes. Mason got on top and knocked him out with a vicious shot to his jaw."

"And then you took Mason out?"

"It was too easy, and he admitted to the dosing. I was so angry. His back was turned to me. I stabbed him with a hunting knife. I just realized how poetic that is." He laughed out loud. "It was the same hunting knife his grandfather had given me all those years ago. The hardest part was dragging that body over the bluff. Then I took the knife and drove it through the agent's heart. The rest was simple. I wrapped the agent's hand around the knife for fingerprints and voila. The renewed grief I felt over my beautiful Corrina's death made my recounting of the events of that morning all the more convincing."

"We had that team out there looking for the second murder weapon for three days," Noble sounded.

"I should've listened to my intuition. Geno was right, and you even said it, kid, 'Doc isn't here and we might be looking for a third guy'." Barnes' frustration reflected in his voice.

"What's done is done, gentlemen. You now have almost everything you need." Nichols put his hands back on the piano keys. "But things have become a bit more interesting."

Barnes dropped his head. "They have the girl. She's been here the whole time, hasn't she?"

"Yes, Detective, you catch on quickly." Nichols plinked at the piano slowly. "They have Reagan and three others and you're running out of time." Merrily, Merrily, Merrily, Merrily…

He felt the wind exit his body as his lungs compressed. Reagan, the missing case he'd given Patricia, the department of justice.

"Partner, are you okay" Noble recognized the impact of the doc's statement on Barnes.

"Doc, why are you involved in this? What did they have on you?"

Nichols finished the melody on the piano…"Life is but a dream." He reached into his lap, pulled a revolver out, held it to his temple, and pulled the trigger.

CHAPTER 40

Barnes paced on the phone with Agent Trent as they watched the coroner wheel the bag out of the house and slide it into the wagon. *Another dead body to contend with.* This time, there was no fighting the urge. He took out his emergency cigarette and slipped it between his lips. It felt as if it had never left. The relief was almost instantaneous. He took three deep drags and held it in for half a minute, enjoying the taste.

"Crap," Noble whistled. "What the heck was that? I can't believe that just happened."

Barnes exhaled slowly and watched as the smoke swirled in front of them. "Twenty-six years on the force. You never get used to seeing something like that."

"I don't understand?" Noble shook his head. "One minute, the guy is sitting there picking music notes on the piano, and then he just blows his head off?"

"It was a soul cleansing." Barnes took another drag of his cigarette. "He couldn't escape his involvement. But worse than that, he knew it contributed to Corrina's death. That was a burden he could not continue to carry. She was the one real thing he had in his life. Giving us that info was probably a last shot at some kind of atonement before he pulled the trigger."

"But just like that? Right in front of us?" Noble was still reckoning with the harsh ending.

"In a way, we were fortunate." Barnes was introspective. "He was going to do that, regardless. We got more than we asked for."

"I suppose I'm still struggling with the doc's involvement in this?" Noble sat on the edge of the fountain. "I mean, come on, he was a valued member of our community, a doctor, for crying out loud. He had a beautiful home, a beautiful wife, a beautiful life. Why would he do this?"

"Experience has taught me a lot on this job." The aging detective paused, taking a spot next to his partner. "Everybody smiles for the camera, Colt. We have no way of knowing what is going on in someone's head or behind closed doors."

"Yeah, I guess so," Noble accepted. "Did you get Trent up to speed?"

Barnes inhaled another chest full of thick cigarette smoke. "Yeah, he's giving us 24 hours and then he's calling in reinforcements."

"He can't do that," Noble responded. "This is our case."

"You heard the doc, Colt…they've got four live girls with them as hostages." He eyeballed the cigarette, watching it burn brightly as he inhaled. "Trent should've called in support right away. He's staying as true to his word as possible."

"Then we've got to get by the Crown and get this guy in custody," Noble suggested.

"Trent confirmed the Walkers have checked out. The senator's wife is on the plane flying back home with her son's remains."

Colton looked at him. "Almost sounds like we're being watched. And 24 hours doesn't give us much time. You have any ideas on how to find this crooked prick?"

"No, but I've got an idea where to look." Barnes pulled the butt of the cigarette out of his mouth, looked at it, and flung it into the wind. "I'm guessing our friend, Sable, knows more than she's telling."

"Okay, but should we poke around here a bit before we hightail it out?"

"We're short on time, Colt." Barnes looked back toward the house. "Why don't you go through the place and I'll head out to the strip joint."

"You sure about this?"

"We need every spare second we can get."

"Roger that." Colt extended his hand toward his partner. "Let's get this dirty sleazeball."

Barnes shook it with a firm grip. "Roger that."

CHAPTER 41

Signposts, streetlights, and traffic signals went by unnoticed as, deep in thought, Barnes raced his car toward an unannounced meeting with the Lovergirls owner, Miss Sable. The winds were gusting again, and the dark clouds dumped rain in the form of heavy droplets that almost bounced off of the windshield with a drumming thump.

He thought back to the first meeting, how her voice had changed once the security guard was excused and left the room. She seemed more cooperative. He wondered why.

Headed north on Pacific Coast Highway past the sandy bluffs and the trail leading to the lighthouse. He passed by the beach and thought he noticed a small rim of clear sky on the horizon.

Rose's Diner was already far out of his rearview mirror when he made the turn and took the winding two-lane highway away from the quiet beach town. He settled in for the 45-minute ride to the edge of the county. The more he drove, the more impatient he became. *What was it the doc had said? 'You won't catch him…you don't know what you're up against?'* He wanted the senator behind bars so badly, he could taste it. *And now he's got Reagan? The girl was basically the catalyst for this entire journey. I didn't find her...Patricia may have figured this whole thing out, but she's gone and it's my fault.*

The urge for another cigarette became intense. Fumbling through the interior, he hoped to get lucky, just one...maybe the last guy in this vehicle left one behind. There was nothing in the center console or tucked in the visor. He was about to reach for the glove compartment when his phone went off.

"Colt," he barked angrily into the device.

"Everything okay, Brad?"

"Yeah, I'm just having a moment," Barnes calmed. "What's up?"

"You will not believe this crap," Noble hinted.

"Running low on patience, kid, there's a clock ticking." Barnes sighed.

"I'm sorry, Brad." Noble refocused. "Nichols left it all open for us to find. He's got a subterranean floor the size of a grand ballroom down there."

"Not a crime, kid."

"Gimme a minute to finish, will ya?" exasperation filled Colt's voice. "There's a hallway that runs on the outside of the giant circular room. There were seven doors, I couldn't get them open. It took me a while to figure it out, but I found a panel with switches. When I pushed the right button, walls opened to the center, and you could see into the rooms behind glass barriers."

"What are you talking about?" Barnes pressed.

"He kept the girls there. A bed in every room, cameras, I don't know, maybe online porn? Maybe just monitoring? Brad, I think this…"

"It was a bidding room." Barnes put together another piece of the puzzle. "Those parties, the pictures with the high-profile politicians, the foreign dignitaries, the rich and depraved. He and the senator used his charities as a front."

"I don't understand…a bidding room?"

"Yeah, they call all these rich people from other countries here under the guise of charity. When the party thins out, these 'special' people retreat to the underground theater to look the merchandise over. They bid against each other for the property to take home."

"Brad, we gotta get this scumbag!" Noble hissed into the phone.

"Look for a surveillance room, tapes, hard drives, whatever you can find," Barnes ordered. "But listen to me, kid. You keep it, only you, understand?"

Noble sighed. "I'm on it, partner."

"And, Colt." He slammed the glove box shut, no cigarette. "Nice job over there, kid, marvelous job."

"It's not over yet, Brad…"

"Well aware of that. I'm pulling into the club now. Keep you posted." Barnes clicked off.

He walked into the club with a spring in his step. Answers were what he was after, and it was his intention to get them and fast. The bartender recognized him and was already punching numbers into the keypad of the phone. "I haven't seen her yet today and there's no answer."

"You're telling me she's not here?" the detective pressed.

"No, I'm telling you I haven't seen her, and she's not answering the phone." The bartender held a blank stare. "That's what I know."

Barnes looked up towards the 'den' and took a long glance around the interior, resting on the huge security guard who had ushered them up on the previous visit. "Let me ask you something, bud."

"Can't guarantee I'll be able to answer. Job security, you understand..."

"You got a cigarette?" he sat on the stool.

The bartender pulled a few out of his red and white box of smokes and handed them to the detective. "Here you go, take a couple of extras. You look like you need them more than I do."

"The night is young, my friend." Barnes regarded him questioningly, "Matches?"

He tossed a small box of stick matches to the beleaguered cop. While looking at the cover, he caught it in the air and paused. An ironic chuckle escaped. "Somehow, even something as tender as a simple kiss can be turned into something ugly." The same matchbox was on the dead bouncer at the beach.

"What's that?" the bartender asked.

"Nothing, mind if I smoke?" Barnes asked, striking the tip along the side and lighting the cigarette.

"Guess not." The bartender clinked some glasses behind the counter.

"Is it normal for her to miss work?"

"She's been busy the past couple of days. But I'd say no, she rarely misses work." The bartender dried his hands.

"You have a number for her?" Barnes smiled snidely. Before the drink jockey replied, Barnes felt his phone vibrate on the counter. It wasn't Colt unless he was calling from the doc's landline. "Hello, Detective Barnes."

"Hello, Detective, this is Agent Wright."

CHAPTER 42

"What can I do for you, Agent Wright?" It did not catch Barnes off guard. "I don't presume you are calling me to tell me you are bringing the senator in?"

"Now, why would I do something like that?" He snickered. "The senator has done nothing unlawful."

"Of course, he hasn't." Barnes laughed. "The line's not tapped, Agent Wright. Is there something I can answer for you?"

"No, but there is something you can do for yourself," Wright expressed in his unnerving monotone voice.

Barnes exhaled into the phone. "And what precisely would that be?"

"The senator would prefer to meet with you to consider the case."

"And if I decline?" Barnes challenged, signaling to the bartender for a beer.

"If you decline, the consequences might be fatal, Detective," Wright was direct.

Barnes held his response for a few moments. "You mean for the senator's career, right, Agent Wright? You aren't threatening an appointed officer of justice, are you?"

"I think the time for games is over, don't you, Detective?" Wright's bitter tone rang clear. "By fatal, I mean for you, Detective, and perhaps your partner."

Barnes considered his reply. He knew he should not show fear. "Well, I'm not too concerned for my health at this point, and my partner, he's tough as nails. Just ask those clowns you sent to the Nest to take us out."

He felt but ignored the dig. "Detective, I urge you to listen to the senator. We can still work this out with no further repercussions and possibly to your benefit," Wright offered.

"I'm fairly certain that the senator is only obsessed with his benefit, or we wouldn't be here." Barnes recognized the need to get under the senator's skin and was sure he was monitoring. "Of course, you can always turn tail and run like the cowards you are and hope to dodge this bullet. But the senator can't fix everything, can he?"

Agent Wright was silent, but his heavy breathing could easily be distinguished. "Then you have forced our hand, Detective. We have hostages. Hostages that will be killed if you do not meet the senator's demands."

"Would that be the four girls you seized from Nichols' residence?"

He was right. The senator was tapped in and was growing furious at Barnes' indignation.

Agent Wright paused for some time. "I'm not sure what you are alluding to, but does it matter where they came from? What should matter to you is where they are going if you do not follow..."

The senator couldn't take anymore of Barnes' chiding. "Here's how this is going to go, Detective. You'll meet me at the lighthouse. You and me. If I get the hint of any other involvement or if you are late, I'll disappear, and you'll never know I was there. In addition, there will be four more dead bodies for you to reckon with. This afternoon at 5:30 pm, we'll be watching. Do not tell anyone. Come unarmed. This can still come to an amicable close. There will be no further communication. Their blood is on your hands, Detective."

Barnes looked at his phone. It was already 4:30 pm.

CHAPTER 43

O ftentimes, we don't realize we've crossed the line until we're on the other side of it.

Barnes was positive this was a bad idea. He knew he should've called Trent or Agent Mills and asked for support. There should have been a plan, but this kind of thinking should've taken place long before he found himself on the path, halfway to the lighthouse. There was not enough time anyway, and there was no turning back now. He left the burner phone Mills issued him at Lovergirls. He did not contact Colton. Against his better judgement, he was going in alone.

It's true, he could've called in the Cavalry. Meeting with the senator in the lighthouse was a stupid move. But if he didn't show up, he was sure there would be four more unnecessary deaths to contend with. More importantly, he was also certain that he needed to catch the senator with his hands in the cookie jar. He had convinced himself that he owed Patricia that much.

Walker could not be aware of the information they had, or he wouldn't have put himself in a situation where his only escape route was through the detective and back across that bluff. *Unless it was a trap or maybe a deception?*

That line of reasoning disappeared when he saw Agent Wright standing guard at the entrance of the tower door. Flown in under cover of twilight and skimming the tops of the waves, a huge black helicopter rested on the bluff next to the lighthouse, almost invisible except for the heavy rotor blades against the last light in the sky.

It didn't matter anymore; this was now between Barnes and the senator. Reagan, the missing girl, and the link to Patricia had turned this into a personal war. Senator Walker's arrogance and overconfidence turned it into a vendetta. The fact that he felt he could not be caught and was above the law propelled him like jet fuel. One way or the other, it was going to end here.

A face-to-face with the corrupt politician was just what the doctor ordered, so to speak. The idea that he had to meet at the lighthouse was the only drawback in the scenario.

Halfway over the bluff, the wind whipped with a frenzy. His thick grey hair blew wildly and the trench coat he wore flapped loudly against his legs, catching the gusts, almost moving him across the path. He's reached the narrow part of the trail, where the cliffs and the rusted guardrails that once promised protection had long since eroded. Seventy feet below, the craggy rocks and punishing tide beckoned. Waves blasted the cliff, and the strong gusts carried water and mist high over the edge, pelting the detective as he walked.

That didn't seem to bother the seagulls whose wings danced on the wind, he noticed. His pace slowed and he scooted along, back to the chain-link fence. He clenched his fingers around the thin metal to keep him away from the dangerous precipice and a certain plunge to death.

Wright had been monitoring the detective and simultaneously surveying the area while communicating with his security people to ensure Barnes was alone. The agent opened the door and called to the senator, "He's almost here, sir. I still think this is a mistake. I can put a bullet in him quietly. We should get on that chopper and distance ourselves from this now. It'll be cleaner that way."

"Not a stinking chance, my friend. That cocky punk detective needs to know that he's lost and see who he's lost to. And I want to see the look on his face when he realizes it."

"But, sir, we can operate quicker and with more authority from our own turf," the agent argued.

"You will not take this from me!" the senator bellowed. "That little pissant cannot challenge me and walk away unscathed. Send him up."

Wright looked back at the trail and watched as the detective made his way past the treacherous, narrow trail onto more sure footing. Barnes took a moment to catch his breath before continuing.

One hundred and fifty more feet and Barnes had reached the lighthouse. His legs were still a bit shaky from the narrow cliffhanger when Agent Wright asked him to relinquish any weapons and then patted him down. He then swung the door open and, pointing upward, allowed the detective into the five-floor structure.

A large room surrounded by two-foot-wide brick walls welcomed the main level. A cast-iron shell, 1.5 inches thick, erected on the outside of the structure did not touch the bricks.

This was a defense for internal residents against lightning strikes.

Rich hand-woven rugs lay over polished hard wood floors. Victorian-style furniture, chairs, a sitting couch, a small table, and a larger desk lined along the walls, all surrounding a wood-burning stove with a chimney that vented to the outside. Oil paintings of tall ships at sea and waves crashing on the beach hung on the walls. The town committee for refurbishing the old place had done a fantastic job. Barnes was feeling the effects of the cold winter storm and wished the stove was operational. He dumped the trench coat in favor of the flexibility of movement despite the biting cold.

A spiral staircase led to the next level and, since the senator was nowhere in sight, Barnes made his way up into the kitchen. They had remodeled this with newer technology and were clearly ready for the next step of turning the lighthouse into a bed-and-breakfast-style experience.

With no senator in view, he continued up the staircase into the living quarters where one-half of the level housed a huge queen-sized poster bed and the other a set of bunks for any children to rest. The décor had returned to a more Victorian version.

"Up one more flight, Detective," Barnes heard the senator sigh.

He looked up the narrowing staircase and a small feeling of claustrophobia hit him. How did anybody live in these things? He didn't consider himself a superstitious man but didn't like the feeling when, in a matter of 13 steps, the stairs ended, and he came through the opening. It was there that he saw the senator sitting in a chair in the log room, pouring a small bottle of vodka into a plastic cup. There was another cup on the desk where the lighthouse keepers would log the weather, temperature, conditions, and any ships that passed by when the place was operational.

Winslow pointed to the other chair and indicated he should take a seat. "Would you care to join me?"

"Oh, what the heck," Barnes figured. *You only live once,* he thought of Patricia. His nerves were on edge when he looked out a small window and realized how high they were. That, coupled with the worrisome trek, left him a bit wobbly. "Make it a double."

The senator laughed and pulled another motel-sized bottle out of his jacket. "These aren't cheap, you know."

"I'm sure you can afford it." Barnes was cold. He looked up where a shorter wood ladder led to a closed weather hatch. "Where are the girls?"

"It's like that, huh?" The senator gave a crooked smile. "No pleasantries at all?"

"I'm not in the mood to be pleasant, Senator." He swallowed a small mouthful.

"Shame, I hoped this might go more smoothly." Winslow downed his vodka and eyed the detective. He wanted to leverage the situation. "Very well, they're up above, waiting to find out what your decision on their life is."

Barnes heard Patricia's voice again…*Go slow.* "Why don't we get to the point, Senator?"

"Maybe you're not aware of your position, Detective?" The arrogance oozed. "No matter what you do, you will lose, and I will win."

Barnes was indignant. "Is that so?"

"Yes, Detective. You see, I have the power, I have the position, and I have the money." His voice became authoritative. "I can control the narrative and I can dictate the outcome."

"I fail to see why you need anything from me then?" Barnes was smug. He wanted to make the senator emotional, off-balance.

"I don't need you or anything from you or anyone else, you little..." He calmed himself with deep breaths.

"Of course not. You can dictate the outcome." Barnes sat back and crossed his legs.

"Yes, I can!" he shouted. "I can do whatever I want, don't you understand?"

Barnes extended his hand and picked under his fingernails. "Then exactly why did you want to talk with me?"

"You are an annoying little cocksucker..." The senator leaned forward. "I'm trying to help you."

"Help me?" Barnes laughed. "What are you talking about?"

"If you could stop acting like a jackass and listen, I'll make everything clear," the senator barked.

Barnes motioned to zip his lips.

"There are two paths here, Detective." Winslow began, "The path of least resistance goes through you. In my estimation, it would be beneficial to all parties concerned if you wrap this beach situation up as a homicide. A crime of passion over a jilted lover."

"And you're okay with Mason taking the fall?" Barnes pinched.

"You still think this is some kind of game, don't you?" The senator was growing tired of the nonsense but knew he needed the detective's cooperation. "Okay, that's not the outcome I'd envisioned, but it's negotiable if that moves you to a more amicable position?"

"That's it?" Barnes snickered. "That's your big plan? That's what you made me walk that death path over the cliffs for?"

The senator's eyes were burning a hole in the detective's forehead, but he kept his cool. "Of course not, there's more. You recover these four lost girls and return them to their families. You and your partner are heroes. Then you turn around and pin their disappearance on the strip club owner, Miss Sable, and her trafficking ring. You do not name Mason with any involvement in the ring. We close up shop here permanently, and as long as no one is the wiser, you walk with a million in cash."

"And Miss Sable is okay with taking the fall for you?"

"She'll be paid quite handsomely," Walker Jr. indicated.

"More like she'll be too dead to refute the charges." Barnes wasn't finished agitating the senator and smiled. "And what's behind door number two?"

"You insolent suck." The senator was fuming. "I'll tell you what's behind door number two, you ungrateful prick. I just offered you the Lombardi trophy, the Stanley cup, and you mock me? Behind door number two, I shoot these girls in front of you, one by one. And then shoot you after you watch them die. I put your fingerprints on the weapon." Spittle was shooting from his mouth. His lips quivered uncontrollably, and his face had turned beet red. He'd edged to the seat of his chair to get into the face of the detective. "This clusterfuck crime scene will leave everyone scratching their heads. Even if someone could tie it to Mason, it would never get back to me. And even then, it'd be tied up in litigation forever, but I'd be long gone, living on the millions I've banked away. And you? Like that bitch reporter, Martin Bender, when I find him, will be rotting in the ground."

"Do you really think that I would be stupid enough to come here if I didn't know more than you think I know?" Barnes was pulling his best poker face.

"What the fuck are you talking about?" Winslow wiped some saliva from his chin.

"I'm talking about the DOJ, you stupid, cocky, arrogant dirtbag." Barnes couldn't hold back. "I don't give a shit what you do to me. My life ended four months ago when my wife died. My only regret would be that I won't get to see you go on trial and spend the rest of your lousy existence behind bars… with a new boyfriend."

The senator started laughing, hysterically. "You really think you are in control, don't you?"

The suction sound of the hatch being turned and opened at the top of the ladder finally broke the dead silence that filled the room after that statement. A pair of expensive, black

Italian loafers started down the steps, followed by long legs in a dark, pinstriped suit.

"That would be impossible, Brad," came a big booming voice. "There's no way any investigation like that could take place without my knowledge."

Barnes was dumbstruck. "Deputy Director Fairbanks? Your hands are in this?"

CHAPTER 44

He trained his gun on the detective. "Sorry, Brad, I'm sure it's a bitter pill to swallow. Especially since we just shared drinks a few months ago."

"You've got to be kidding me?" Barnes just could not seem to wrap his mind around this recent development. "What about that big speech at the awards banquet? All about the FBI family, how you rose in the ranks, and that galvanizing, team-building 'I've always got your backs' statement?"

"That was good, wasn't it?" Fairbanks chuckled.

"It's no wonder the rest of the free world laughs at America. The left hand always fights the right. The corruption is an epidemic. We can't even trust an election, let alone the nation's leaders," Barnes spat.

"Still the best country in the world, Brad." Fairbanks was stoic. "The people in power will not relinquish it without a fight. And we are among the people in power..." He looked toward the senator.

"Enough of this, 'Banks'. We need to finish this meeting and get back to business."

"Your 'people in power' let a murderer walk away unpunished after killing my wife. Because of an immigration status?" Barnes was about to come unglued. "I trusted you. You promised to give me that intel on the illegal."

"You played football didn't you Brad? It's the old misdirection play."

He extended a long arm toward the senator. "How can you live with yourself, you slime-sucking weasel? You're supposed to go after people like this unlawful fat ogre."

"You know, Brad, I actually liked you when we met that night at the Bonaventure. Dutiful, supportive husband, but with an edge…strong. It did not surprise me when Patricia told me you were a cop. You had that look, that walk, maybe even a confident swagger."

"Strange, I didn't have the same feeling about you. That pompous, bullshit speech of yours seemed totally contrived and unusually self-serving. Did you really think anyone was there to listen to you ramble about your accomplishments?"

"Wind 'er up. We're just wasting our time here." Speaking into a wrist transmitter, Fairbanks reached his limit. "Senator, you were wrong. There are not two paths."

Outside, Agent Wright moved to the helicopter. He tapped on the window and made a circular motion with his hand. The pilot hit the ignition and, slowly, the long blades began to turn.

Fairbanks could hear the engine revving through the open hatch. "This self-righteous little worm is too hardheaded to listen to reason. I'm going to get it right this time. I'll kill him myself."

"Yeah?" Barnes kept digging. "Well, you're zero for two so far. Neither the biker gang nor the cut brake line could get the job done."

"Actually, we're zero for three, Detective." Fairbanks stared into confused eyes.

"It's time for me to go." The senator stood, straightened his coat, and squeezed his way toward the stairs. "I'll leave you to it, 'Banks'. Don't forget the girls." He took a couple of steps down, stopped, and turned toward Barnes. "Detective…"

He looked at the senator.

"Just wanted to see your face when I remind you…I win, you lose." Winslow flipped him the middle finger.

Ignoring him, Barnes was still churning grey matter. "Zero for three? Are you telling me you tried to kill me in the accident with my wife? You sleazy little scumbag…" Barnes stepped toward the deputy director.

"Easy, Brad." Fairbanks shook his head, raising the pistol toward the detective. "Patricia was good, Detective. The promotion and the award were to get her off the trail. But we learned she wouldn't let it go. To make matters worse, she was making progress. She brought it to me and the bureau killed it. Well, actually, I killed it. We figured you knew as much as she did. After all, you're the husband. The accident on the way home from the awards banquet? There was no construction on the freeway that night. Our man, the valet, guided you on the route we hoped you would take. The driver of the utility vehicle was paid handsomely for his service, freed in Mexico, and snuffed out to clean up the loose ends. But he did not get the job done. You were still alive."

Barnes' anger raged inside him. "You set that up? You gutless bitch! You murdered my wife? An FBI agent killing one of their own? And you tried to kill me?" He could not contain his anger and lunged at Fairbanks.

The deputy director fired a shot to the side of Barnes' head and into the bricks, halting his advance.

Barnes wanted a reckoning.

"It was a timing thing." Fairbanks looked at the gun in his hand. "Like this situation, it was kill or be killed. The girl she was investigating escaped. We lost her and the trail Patricia had led to Rocky Point. If the girl turned up here, there would've been no way to control the investigation. Once the wheels were in motion and we made the decision, it was our best chance at containment.

"You have no regard for law or life, do you?" Barnes seethed. He scanned the room, looking for some way to get out of this without being shot. "What about those four innocent girls up there on the light deck? They don't deserve this. At least try to do something right and let them go."

"You should be a comedian." The deputy director laughed. "No, unfortunately, they have seen faces. So, the great Detective Barnes will shoot them. And as the senator pointed out earlier, the focus of this whole mess will shift to you. Everything will be so cattywampus here. We'll have all the time we need to get this thing so cleaned up, there wouldn't be any way to tie us to it."

Barnes wondered what it would feel like to get shot. In all the years on the force, he'd never taken a bullet. His anger burned, but he wasn't scared. He was going to be with Patricia again. *It's where I should've been all along,* he thought.

Before the deputy director could pull the trigger, a powerful gust of wind flipped the hatch shut with a 'slam'. Fairbanks looked up at the ladder for only a brief second and Barnes was on him. He knocked the gun out of his hand and it clunked down the stairs. Lunging, the detective's forehead caught Fairbanks square in the jaw. He bit through his tongue and sprayed a mouthful of blood across the room.

Barnes stepped back and drove a heavy fist into the deputy director's gut, knocking the wind out of him. His hands found their way behind Fairbanks' head, and he slammed it down into his knee, once, twice. He felt the cartilage snap and knew he'd broken his nose. A third time, his rage was uncontrollable. The senator was unconscious before the fourth knee smashed against him. Barnes dropped him on the hardwood floor only long enough to note the immense amount of blood pooling around him.

He was huffing and puffing, anger radiated out of his body. He pulled the deputy director up the ladder by his tie like he was a stuffed animal, and deposited him against the rail overlooking the ocean 100 feet below. Then he turned around. "We'll get you all out of here safely and on your way home in just a minute." He tried to calm the four frightened young teens. "I've got one more thing to do..."

He wanted to push him over the side, wanted to exact all the revenge he was certain he deserved. The thought of watching the deputy director's body catapult over the side and crashing into the craggy rocks below was tantalizing and just a motion away.

But he knew it wouldn't bring Patricia back. He missed that smile, missed her touch, her love. An overwhelming emptiness coursed through him and he suddenly realized how someone could come to the decision to 'jump'. He was back in the front seat of the car again after the accident, talking to Patricia, screaming at her to fight. She looked at him, and even in her unseeing eyes, he saw all of her love. Sitting on the deck with his back against the rail, his heavy head rested in his hands and he sobbed quietly until he heard shrieks.

The girls had alerted him. Fairbanks came to, reached into his pocket, retrieved a knife, and stood over the detective. Barnes didn't hesitate. He twisted, grabbed the deputy director behind his knees, lifted, and Fairbanks went over the side.

As badly as he wanted to watch, he did not. He untied the girls and told them to close and lock the hatch until he returned. He would knock two times, wait, and then two more. Barnes raced down the ladder and down the flight of stairs to find the gun. Three more levels and he pushed the door open and looked at the chopper, his frame a silhouette in the light.

Agent Wright knew in a second it was Barnes. "Get this bird outta here!" he screamed. "Senator, we have a huge mess to clean up."

"Don't worry, son, I'm a sitting United States Senator. I've got this. I can fix anything." Winslow was smug. "I'll see that detective go down if it's the last thing I do."

Barnes drew the pistol, walked casually toward the chopper, and shot at the windshield. The shots hit the target but did not penetrate, only jolting the pilot.

"Get us the fuck out of here!" Wright yelled. The huge chopper lifted off, dropped over the edge, and headed out over the Pacific Ocean.

Barnes fired three more shots that missed wildly. And as the loud thundering of the main rotor and the swash plate receded, he heard shouting and saw the flashlight beams behind him.

"Colt, is that you?" Barnes shouted out.

Noble was racing toward him with agents Trent and Mills close behind, rifles in hand.

"Yeah," he said, out of breath. "The bartender at the strip club heard you mention the lighthouse," Colt answered. "Smart move to leave the phone behind. We tracked it, got us here. What the crap happened?"

"Never mind that, you've got a rifle, can you shoot that thing?" Barnes shouted into the wind. "Target the lights."

Noble wrapped the strap around his forearm, planted his feet square, and tried to steady his breathing. He popped off two shots, then lowered the weapon.

The chopper continued across the water.

"Out of range, huh?" Barnes sighed, watching the chopper continue along.

"That's okay, we'll get 'em. They can't hide any longer," Trent reassured. He brought a huge walkie-talkie to his chin, "We got a bogie skimming waves headed out from the lighthouse. I need eyes on and let me know where they land."

A loud crack then split the night, and the detective saw smoke against the moon's reflection on the waves. Seconds later, the chopper burst into flames, dipped its flight pattern, and exploded into the ocean.

"Shit, kid." Barnes whooped. "Just like the fourth of July."

Noble just smiled calmly and mustered up his best southern accent, "I can shoot."

"You sure can, kid," Agent Mills added. "What're we looking at, who was onboard?"

"Just the senator and his crooked bodyguard. You're with the DOJ, right? Then you should be familiar with this, Agent Mills. We're looking at justice. And it's not going to cost the government a thing or get held up in any legalese. Oh, I almost forgot…there's an added bonus." Barnes put his arm over his partner's shoulder. "Initiation is over, kid. That's for sure."

"I'll need to be completely debriefed, Detective." Agent Trent was smiling.

"My pleasure, Mr. Trent." Barnes laughed. "But first, we've got to get four very frightened young girls off the top of that lighthouse and home to their families."

"It'll be my first order of business, Detective." Trent shook his hand. "You have my word."

"Finally, someone from the government whose word I can trust." Barnes motioned and the four of them headed toward the lighthouse. "Colt, I've got a present for you. Meet me in the morning in the beach parking lot."

On the way, Barnes excused himself and the other three looked on as he walked to the edge of the bluff. He paused and then punched into the air in the direction of the crashed helicopter and screamed at the top of his lungs, "YOU LOSE!"

EPILOGUE

Colton turned into the beach parking lot in the early morning hours and marveled at the beauty that hung behind the clouds as they passed overhead on their way toward the mountains. The sky was bright again, and the storm had almost passed. He could easily have sat there enjoying the change of weather, but he knew they had to be back at the station soon to debrief the DOJ operatives. The case had hit big media and everyone was looking for information… answers.

"Hey, Brad," he yelled after closing the door on his Crown Victoria sedan. "Why are we meeting here, again? You realize we have a big pow-wow to attend."

"Yeah, I know. There's just a bit of unfinished business. Let's take a walk down to the beach," Barnes motioned.

"Yeah, sure. Is everything alright?"

"As fine as it's ever going to be, kid." Barnes brushed his hair back as they headed across the boardwalk and found the sand. "We've got a lot ahead of us…reports, debriefings, press conferences, and likely court appearances as well. I thought we might take a couple of minutes to enjoy the beauty of this place before we head back in."

"I'm okay with that. I could use a little time to reset."

"You know, when I first arrived here, I was already a mess, but getting pulled into this actually helped. Except for the first time I saw Corrina Nichols' picture, I thought I might be coming unglued."

"Yeah, I remember."

"Finally figured out why. Doc told us it wasn't her real name, so I had Eugene do some digging. Her name was actually Amanda Grayson, one of the girls that Mason was treating in Connecticut. The girl that spearheaded the investigation into his business. Her picture probably came in over the wire years ago, and for some reason, stuck with me."

"Wouldn't we have known that in an autopsy?"

"With Nichols' identification, there was no need to dig further."

"Never take things at face value." Noble smiled. "You taught me that."

"Like I said, we're always learning, kid. For the first night since I got here, I slept like a baby. I was exhausted."

"I can imagine. From the way you told it last night, it was quite the event in the lighthouse. I'm sorry I wasn't there." Noble pocketed his hands.

"Would love to have had you there, but they wanted me alone."

"I still can't wrap my arms around a director of the FBI being involved in this."

"It's a crazy time in a crazy world. He had slimeball written all over him, but I never thought he'd be caught up in something like this."

They heard the tires of the coroner's vehicle pull to a stop against the cement parking blocks. Eugene got out and waved.

"What's he doing here?" Noble was confused.

"I remembered you telling me about your 'jumpers' and I could never understand how someone could get to that place. Last night, on that light deck, I was faced with a choice. I wanted to chuck that Fairbanks over the side, to let it out, make it even."

"But you said you didn't, right?"

"That's right. But in that moment, I realized how people become defeated, lost. I thought I let Patricia down and sat there crying. I understood how life can take the fight out of someone. Somehow, I got something back."

"You did the right thing. Anything else would've made you one of them."

"Speaking of them…" Barnes looked over the shoulder of his younger partner. "You said they always ended up in the same place. Right in the middle of the beach."

"I'll be a…is that Fairbanks?" Noble turned and winced.

"Well…most of him anyway." Barnes blinked.

"Was that your present?" Noble watched as Eugene and Clyde headed toward the bloated body floating in the shallow waves with the seaweed.

"No, kid." Barnes reached into his coat and took out his badge. He looked at it for a long moment before handing it to Colton.

"I'm confused. We just took down a major trafficking ring, a corrupt political wing, and got four young girls back to their families, and you're walking away?"

"It's your town now, you've earned it. I can't imagine a more thorough curriculum or graduation ceremony. Trent and Mills wrangled Miss Sable before she got out of dodge. She's turning witness on the rest of the local operation, that includes Mayor Moyer."

"The mayor was involved also?" Noble's jaw dropped. "Man, they got to everyone."

"They're picking him up now along with the three people who raided the therapist's office." Barnes looked up in the direction of the parking lot as another car pulled in.

Noble was somber. "I can't say that this feels much like a present. I thought maybe you were going to give me a letter of recommendation or something."

"That's not the present, Colt. My advice is. I'm going out on a high note. The senator told me he'd given me the Lombardi trophy and he was right...this was the Superbowl of solved cases. But it wasn't me. I remember my wife getting the director's award and how she realized none of us does anything by ourselves. We are all members of a team, and I had a great team. But even the best get passed up by the game. I've made a lot of choices I'm not proud of and I lost one of the only choices I was proud of—my wife. I was married to the job and missed out on too much. Don't make the same mistake, find the right balance. Sara is a good woman, make her your priority."

"I hear you on that." Noble nodded his head. "What are you going to do now?"

"Well, for starters, I'm going to go fishing."

"But you don't like fishing." Noble turned around to catch the councilman striding toward them with a cooler full of cold beer and a couple of long fishing poles.

"It can't be any worse than what we just finished. I reckon I should try to find new ways to relax." Barnes reached into his breast pocket and pulled out a pack of cigarettes. He culled one out and put a match to it. The satisfaction spread across his face instantly. He watched the smoke drift on the soft morning breeze and followed it out over the water. "And occasionally." He took another drag of nicotine and tobacco. "Some of the old ways. I'm certain I've earned that."

"You know," Colton smiled wide. "I think those DOJ guys have enough on their hands for a while…you got an extra pole?"

ACKNOWLEDGEMENTS

Thanks so much for putting the time aside in your busy lives to give this title a look. I do not take your decision to read my book lightly and I'm very hopeful that you enjoyed this read. I'm a 'pantser', not a plotter, which means I sit and type and shape and re-write. I'm quite sure it is a far more difficult approach but until I learn how to plot, I continue in my way. This was another long endeavor and a labor of love, so to speak. I sat on it for some time and then blasted out the entire second half in about two weeks. Go figure.

How do you thank everyone who has your back, supports you, helps keep you focused or moving forward?

With my deepest appreciation: My dearly departed mom, without her encouragement I'd never have even tried. My kids and immediate family, My dream Girl (she knows who she is), Oscar & Amber, Michelle, Cousin Lisa, Scott, Aunt Gaye, Aunt Bonnie, Cheryl, Raz and Pops to whom I owe so much, Shirley, Anita, Teresa, Geoff & Rita, linda@fresh Grace, Keren, Scooter and Pookie (Scott and Maria), Terry, Sam, Faith, Ron and Kalyn and our whole party crew. And if I forgot anyone which I'm sure I have, I apologize and you're included in this: Everyone else I bored with the repetitive discussions and updates of 'my new book' saga.

ABOUT THE AUTHOR

Sean Flynn has not landed on any best seller lists (yet), nor could he be described as a multiple award-winning author. Born and raised in California, he is a father to two awesome young men, a musician, singer, songwriter, digital Graphic artist, writer, author, painter, photographer and a self-professed hopeless romantic. He was once a former jock in the traditional sense, football, basketball and track. He loves skiing and getting warm in cold weather.

His vices include rooting way too hard for the New York football Jets (been a fan all my life), drinking far too much dr. Pepper and killing way too many pizzas.

He looks forward to a time when money is no longer a concern, when he actually has generated enough revenue streams to finally get his act together.

You can visit his Instagram site @authorflynnie or website Https://flynnie.wixsite.COM/author.

THE COLD, HARD FACTS

L et me take this opportunity to thank you for investing in my dream. I didn't know I wanted to write until I tried it. I didn't go to school for it, I just did it.

The competition is fierce. It is estimated that about 600k to 1 million new books are published each calendar year. To even have the hope of selling our products, authors must rely on getting their material in front of readers. One must consider employing at great cost a marketing agency or team of social media experts and influencers to find even a modicum of success, and there are certainly no guarantees.

Self-published authors face an even greater challenge. Reports indicate that the average self-published author will sell at best, 50 copies of their book. That's including family and friends. The cost to self-publish, which includes the time it took to formulate an idea, write the story, obtain a developmental edit, rewrite the story, get another beta read or content edit, rewrite the story again, complete a final draft, submit for a deep copy edit, finalize the manuscript, format the book for release, blurbs and back cover text and get the cover art finished far exceeds the retuned profits on 50 books, or even one thousand for that matter.

Writing books is not easy. Marketing them is far more difficult. Selling them is well, a monumental task at best. You're probably asking yourself a couple of questions as you scan through this…first, why write a book at all if the return-on-investment opportunity is so minimal? And second, and I'm counting on your compassionate, caring and nurturing genetic makeup for this one, is what can you do to help?

The answer to the first question is subjective, we all write for different reasons. For me, it was something I wanted to accomplish. The book SHATTERED was a therapeutic endeavor when my broken heart needed to find a release or coping mechanism, and it became a way that I hoped might reach other broken-hearted people. FROM THE BOTTOM UP was a quest to achieve a personal goal and became a dream that turned into a realization.

The answer to the second question is far simpler. REVIEWS are a major vaulting point, a key that readers utilize to help choose the material they read. The number and nature of quality review drives the algorithm that puts a book title higher up in the queue for prospective buyers to view and therefore consider for purchase.

Make no mistake about it, this is a numbers game all the way around. To improve my chances of getting my work in the hands of prospective readers I need your help. So, if you enjoyed any of the titles you've read, please, please consider leaving a review. I know I'm not asking you to do something that is easy. The truth is most people do not want to be bothered with the task. It takes time and writing a review is not a pleasurable exercise. And worse, I cannot offer you anything in exchange except my deep gratitude. So, I thank you again for purchasing and taking the time to read the books or books and again if you choose to help me further by expanding your appreciation of the work and leaving a review on the purchasing site.

While you're there, please click on the follow the author link so that you are up to date on any future releases.

Thanks, and Have a GOD day!

Made in the USA
Las Vegas, NV
11 February 2023

67319044R00171